"Helping you ... **know you don'** ... **when I say tha** ... **was the last thing I thought I needed."**

She was silent, so he pushed forward, faster now, starting to feel foolish for not just blurting a simple apology and leaving it at that. "That's why I bailed on you when I found out you weren't telling me everything. And when I kissed you..."

Kensie stayed silent, lips pursed like she was waiting for a real apology. Or maybe she wasn't even listening to him. It was hard to tell.

"I'm sorry. I should have—"

"It was a mistake. I get it. I agree. We got carried away in the moment. It's not like it's going to happen again," Kensie said, cutting him off suddenly.

It wasn't going to happen again? Even though that had been his plan, too, hearing her say the words made him long to pull the truck over and see if she really meant it.

Acknowledgments

Thank you to Denise Zaza for suggesting I write a book with a hunky hero and a K-9 partner—I had so much fun creating Colter and Rebel! To everyone involved behind the scenes with *K-9 Defense*—I appreciate everything you do. Finally, thank you to my family and friends, who are always willing to lend their support on my crazy writing journey. Special thanks to Kevan Lyon, Andrew Gulli, Chris Heiter, Robbie Terman, Kathryn Merhar, Caroline Heiter, Ann Forsaith, Charles Shipps, Sasha Orr, Nora Smith and Mark Nalbach.

K-9 DEFENSE

ELIZABETH HEITER

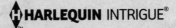

Over the years, I've been lucky enough to have many loyal
companions like Rebel. This book is for all my furry,
feathered and scaled family members.

ISBN-13: 978-1-335-64086-4

K-9 Defense

Copyright © 2019 by Elizabeth Heiter

Recycling programs
for this product may
not exist in your area.

Printed in U.S.A.

www.Harlequin.com

Elizabeth Heiter likes her suspense to feature strong heroines, chilling villains, psychological twists and a little romance. Her research has taken her into the minds of serial killers, through murder investigations and onto the FBI Academy's shooting range. Elizabeth graduated from the University of Michigan with a degree in English literature. She's a member of International Thriller Writers and Romance Writers of America. Visit Elizabeth at www.elizabethheiter.com.

Books by Elizabeth Heiter

Harlequin Intrigue

K-9 Defense

The Lawmen: Bullets and Brawn

Bodyguard with a Badge
Police Protector
Secret Agent Surrender

The Lawmen

Disarming Detective
Seduced by the Sniper
SWAT Secret Admirer

Visit the Author Profile page at Harlequin.com.

CAST OF CHARACTERS

Colter Hayes—In a single moment, Colter Hayes lost everything: his marine brothers, his job, even partial mobility. Now he's hiding and healing in Alaska with his combat tracker dog, Rebel. When Rebel saves the life of outsider Kensie Morgan, Colter sees in her everything he's ever wanted—but knows now he'll never have.

Kensie Morgan—For fourteen years, Kensie has been searching for the sister who was abducted right in front of her. She travels to Alaska on a long-shot lead, but she's ill-prepared to face the natural perils—or her distracting attraction to Colter.

Rebel—Colter's loyal companion was a marine K-9 until she and Colter were injured in the ambush that killed the rest of their unit.

Alanna Morgan—In the years since Kensie's younger sister was kidnapped, leads have dried up. But Kensie has never given up on finding her.

Henry Rollings—No one knows much about the reclusive local, but Kensie is certain he's hiding something about Alanna. The problem is, no one can tell her how to find him to get answers.

Danny Weston—He offers to help Kensie find Alanna, but Danny may not be what he seems.

Chapter One

"I'm still alive."

Three simple words in a note. A note signed by the sister Kensie Morgan hadn't seen in fourteen years had sent her in a frantic rush across 3,500 miles. Kensie had left a brief message on her boss's voice mail, telling him she needed some time off, then called her family. They'd been less supportive.

But this time, Kensie had to believe, the lead could be real.

The hope had buoyed her from one layover to the next, warmed her as she stepped off the plane in Alaska. For early October, the temperature was way colder than she'd expected, and it had only gotten worse as she'd paid for her rental pickup truck and headed north.

Desparre, Alaska, was the kind of place you came to to drop off the map. The sort of place no one would think to look—and even if they did, they might never make it out.

After her GPS had given up and she'd made a

half dozen wrong turns, she'd finally been able to get directions from a local into town. Now Kensie shivered as she stepped out of her truck for the first time in four hours. Her heavy down jacket was no match for the windchill, so she tugged up the collar as strong gusts whipped her long hair around her face. There was no avoiding the snow covering the walkways, so Kensie trudged through it. Her next stop after the police station was going to be for a new pair of boots.

Her fingers tingled from the cold and she clenched them into tight fists in her pockets, hoping the motion would also ease her nerves. She'd planned to make the store where her sister's note had been found her first stop, but when she couldn't find it, she'd given up and headed into the main part of town.

Kensie glanced around, taking in the assortment of buildings—post office, clothing store, bar, drug store, grocery store, church. She felt like she'd stepped back in time to the eighteen hundreds. The only thing missing was horse-drawn carriages. But it was probably too cold for horses. Even the monstrous all-weather truck parked up the street seemed ill prepared for Desparre once winter descended.

Chicago got cold, but after not even one day in Desparre she was longing for the ridiculously cold-but-not-*this*-cold windchill off the lake.

With the exception of a guy playing with his

dog down the road, she was the only fool outside. Kensie hustled, careful not to slide in the snow as she yanked open the door to the tiny police station. Her stomach churned as reality set in. She was finally here.

This time will be different, she told herself, trying to bolster her courage.

The officer behind the counter looked up as she entered, but she wasn't sure if the scowl on his face was for her or the blast of cold air she brought inside. "Can I help you?"

Desparre probably didn't get a lot of outsiders, so she was going to stand out here. Kensie had gotten the same questioning looks each time she'd stopped to ask for directions on the outskirts of town.

If her sister Alanna really was here, maybe she'd be the one to find Kensie.

If only it could be that easy. But fourteen years of bright, painful hope drawn out for days or years and then dashed in yet another dead end, in yet another godforsaken town, told her that nothing about finding Alanna would be easy.

But if the note was real…

The hope that bloomed inside her now brought tears to her eyes.

The officer stood and rushed to her side. "Are you okay? Do you need help?"

She blinked the tears back and prayed her voice

would be steady. "I need to talk to someone about the note you found from Alanna Morgan."

Frown lines dug deeper, creating grooves across the officer's forehead. He looked like he belonged in a rocking chair with a couple of grandkids on his knee, not wearing a police uniform. "Why?"

"I'm her sister."

The flash of emotions on his face was quick, so quick Kensie might have missed them if she hadn't seen them so many times in her life. Surprise, discomfort and pity first. Then something hard and distant—law enforcement probably learned to compartmentalize to keep themselves from going crazy case after case, victim after victim.

"You shouldn't have come all this way. Didn't you talk to the FBI?"

The FBI had spoken to her and her family, of course. They'd been the ones to call and inform Kensie about the note found in Desparre in the first place. But that didn't matter. "I needed to see for myself."

The frown was back, this time mixed with worry, but the officer nodded, patted her on the arm and then said, "I'll be right back."

He disappeared through a door marked Police Only and Kensie took a deep breath.

You can do this, she reminded herself. She was just out of practice. It had been years since the last lead on Alanna.

Standing in a police station now took her back to her childhood. All those years of waiting in hard plastic chairs, her mom's hand clutching hers way too tight, as they prayed for any shred of good news. Her dad standing stiffly beside them, his arm wrapped around her brother, holding him close as if that could keep him safe. Officers catching her gaze and then looking quickly away. Kensie's palms damp and her heart thudding way too fast.

Missing Alanna. Knowing it was all her fault her little sister was gone.

"Ma'am?"

Kensie looked up, realizing her eyes had glazed over as she'd stared at the floor, getting lost in her past. She stiffened her shoulders, tried to look like the professional woman she'd become instead of the terrified thirteen-year-old who always reappeared whenever she heard Alanna's name.

She held out a cold hand, shook hard and stared the new officer directly in the eye. Let her know she couldn't be sent off with a "sorry" and a pat on the back.

"I'm Chief Hernandez."

From the slight grin the chief gave, Kensie's surprise probably showed. She was young for a police chief, likely only a few years older than Kensie's twenty-seven.

But there was wisdom in her steady gaze and strength in her handshake.

"Kensie Morgan. I want to see the note that was left at the store."

Chief Hernandez held out her other hand and Kensie reached for the computer paper.

It was a photocopy, but her heart beat faster at the slanted cursive handwriting. She read it aloud. "My name is Alanna Morgan, from Chicago. I'm still alive. I'm not the only one."

"You recognize the writing?" the chief asked, skepticism in her voice.

"Alanna's? No." How could she? Her sister had been five years old when she'd been kidnapped out of their front yard. At five, everything had been big sloppy letters, forming words that were often misspelled. There was no way to know what Alanna's handwriting looked like now. If she was really still alive, she'd be nineteen.

Nineteen. The very idea made pain and longing mingle. What would a nineteen-year-old Alanna look like? What had happened in all the years between? Kensie had missed all of her sister's milestones.

Focus on now, Kensie reminded herself. *Focus on what you can change.* "What do you know?"

Chief Hernandez shrugged, then frowned, like she regretted the motion. "Not much, I'm afraid. We don't know who left it. We can't be sure it's even real. It says—"

"I know," Kensie cut her off, not wanting to

hear a repeat of the FBI's depressing analysis. "But you must know something. What about the store owner who found it?"

"It was in a stack of bills. He couldn't even say who put it there or when."

Chief Hernandez tilted her head in what Kensie had long ago come to recognize as a pity gesture. "I'm sorry. You came a long way for nothing."

The tears surprised her. They rushed hard and fast to her eyes and Kensie ducked her head, trying to blink them back.

"Miss Morgan—"

"Thanks," she said, handing back the photocopy of the evidence—the photocopy of what might be her little sister's writing. Without another word, she rushed out the door.

This time, the cold was just what she needed. It slammed into her face, stinging her eyes and probably freezing the tears on her cheeks.

Get it together, she told herself. Ducking her head against the wind, she hurried for her rental, parked across the street.

It didn't matter what the police thought. It didn't matter what the FBI thought. It only mattered what her heart was screaming.

Alanna was still alive. And Kensie might finally be able to bring her home.

The gunning of an engine ripped her from her

hopeful thoughts. Her head jerked up and right, toward the source of the sound.

A station wagon the size of a small boat was plowing down the street, spraying snow and coming straight for her.

COLTER HAYES DIDN'T know what happened.

One second, his retired Military Working Dog, Rebel, was goofing off, chasing a stick as naturally as she'd once tracked dangerous bombers back to their hideouts. The next, she was racing away from him so fast he knew her injured leg would be acting up later.

He heard the engine a second after that, spotted the old station wagon careening around the corner, cutting through the slippery snow way too fast. And a woman frozen in the middle of the street.

"Move!" he screamed at the woman, cursing the injury in his own leg—sustained at the same time as Rebel's—as he raced for both of them.

He'd never make it in time.

The world around him seemed to move in slow motion as panic shot up his throat, mingling with the cold and making it hard to breathe. The car slip-sliding out of control. His five-year-old Malinois–German shepherd mix—the only friend he had left in the world—running straight in front of it.

Colter pushed his leg as hard as he could, trying to follow, trying to be of any use at all. But it was no good.

Rebel leapt up high, slamming into the woman's chest with her front legs, knocking both of them out of sight as the car raced past Colter. It slowed for a second, then sped off.

The panic dropped lower, making his chest hurt and his heart beat too fast. The memory of a year ago, of Rebel jumping on him as a bullet passed so close he felt its trajectory over his head, made it hard to breathe.

He tried to push it out of his mind, willed himself not to fall into that darkness as he raced across the street, sliding in the snow toward the two figures lying prone on the ground. He dropped to his knees, ignoring the *pop* in his knee and the pain that rushed up his thigh.

Another memory from a year ago, of surgery after surgery as he begged to know the condition of his unit. No one would tell him.

Colter blinked the present back into focus.

Rebel climbed off the woman, her movements a little stiff. She nudged her way under his arm, like she knew he was hurt.

Colter dug one hand into the soft fur on Rebel's back, reassuring himself she hadn't been hit.

Still lying flat, the woman groaned and reached a trembling hand up to the back of her head, poking around like she was searching for blood. But her hand came back clean and he helped her to a sitting position.

She stared at him with haunting brown eyes framed by dark lashes. Long, silky dark hair slid over her shoulders and across the back of his hand. The kind of woman he wouldn't have been able to resist once upon a time.

But she was as stupid as she was gorgeous.

"What were you thinking? Crossing the road without paying any attention?" His voice rose even as Rebel pushed her wet nose into his neck, something that usually made him laugh.

But nothing could make him laugh today. "You almost got yourself killed. You almost got my dog killed!"

"I'm so sorry," she whispered, sounding more shell-shocked than scared at her near miss. She reached a still-trembling hand out toward Rebel, gently stroking his dog's brown-and-black fur.

Rebel ate it up, the little traitor, giving the woman a solid push with her nose as if to ask for more.

The woman laughed, a deep, rich sound that seemed to curl around his body.

Colter scowled at both of them, but tried to keep his anger in check. Stupid or not, she had almost died a few minutes ago. And she wasn't a soldier in battle, but a civilian clearly out of place in Alaska.

To his surprise, his voice came out calm, almost

soothing. "Let's get you out of the street before another car comes through. Everyone's going too fast today. Living here, they *should* know how to drive in the snow, but with the first snowfall of the season, it's like everyone forgets."

"Thanks," she whispered in that same soft, slightly husky voice.

It would have been a voice for his dreams, back when he had dreams. These days it was nothing but nightmares.

"Come on, girl," he told Rebel as he planted his hands in the snow and pushed himself clumsily to his feet.

"Are you okay?" the woman asked, her eyes even wider than they'd been a minute ago.

"Yeah, fine." It felt like his knee was on fire, but experience told him it didn't warrant a trip to the doctor. He'd just twisted it wrong and the rod and screws holding together his right thigh didn't appreciate it.

He had a few nights of ice and elevation in his future, but he'd been through worse. Much worse.

"I'm so sorry." Her voice wobbled, like she was on the verge of tears.

He prayed she'd keep them in check. "It's not your fault. It's a war injury." He held out a hand to help her up, but she frowned at it, climbing slowly to her feet on her own.

Colter felt his face redden. At six foot two and 180 pounds of mostly muscle—even after his injury—people had always looked to him for help physically. The snub now hurt more than the hit to his knee had.

Once they were safely on the sidewalk, she shuffled her feet. She shoved her hands into the pockets of her too-thin coat, another dead giveaway she wasn't from around here. It looked warm enough, but it wasn't cut out for Desparre's coming winter.

Her gaze darted from him to Rebel and then off into the distance, as if she was afraid he was going to yell at her again.

Colter held in a sigh. Beautiful or not, he didn't have the energy to coddle her. But she was starting to tremble, and he figured it was as much the realization of her near miss setting in as the cold. So he tried for a smile.

It felt unnatural, as if those muscles had forgotten how to work, but she seemed to relax a little. "I'm Colter Hayes. And this is Rebel."

She held out her hand. "Kensie Morgan."

He had her hand in a firm grip before the last name sank in. It had been all over the news a few weeks ago. "Morgan. As in—"

"Yes. I'm Alanna Morgan's sister. I came here to find her."

Although he could feel the tremble in her hand, her voice was strong, almost daring him to challenge her ability. Not that he'd dare. If there was one thing he understood, it was loyalty to a sibling, blood related or not.

And hope. He understood how hope could keep you going, when everything inside you screamed it was time to give up. "I hope you do find her."

"Thanks," she replied as he reluctantly let go of her hand. "Rebel is amazing. I froze and then she just—she saved my life."

"She was a military dog. A Gunnery Sergeant, in fact." One rank higher than his own, because the military taught soldiers to respect their K-9 partners.

"Really?" Kensie's gaze dipped to Rebel, whose tail wagged as they talked about her.

"Yeah." He didn't know why he'd shared that. Now that Kensie was looking less shaken up, he needed to get out of there. Away from the intensity in her eyes and the fullness of her lips. Away from the sudden physical attraction that took him by surprise.

"What did she do in the military?"

"Combat Tracker Dog," Colter said quickly, knowing that, like most people, she'd probably have no idea what that meant. "You should get out of the cold. You're not dressed for Desparre."

Even though her lips were taking on the slightest tinge of blue, she didn't seem to notice the cold—or his suggestion—as she stared at Rebel. "Tracker?"

There was too much hope in her voice. A dozen

swear words lodged in Colter's brain. "Not that kind of tracker."

"But what—"

"She tracked back to perpetrators from explosion sites." Just saying the words filled his mind up with images of a military convoy, blown to bits. Bomb fragments lodged in everything. Limbs not attached to people. Friends, gone in an instant.

An L-shaped ambush that had come in two waves, one for the people he'd come to help and one for the responders. His chest started to compress again, the edges of his vision dulling.

"But couldn't she—"

"No," Colter snapped, more harshly than he'd intended.

Even if he and Rebel did the kind of tracking she wanted, she had no idea what she was asking. If he tried to help her, he knew what would happen. He'd have a mission again. A reason to reconnect with the world.

And connections meant pain.

"I'm sorry," he added over his shoulder as he spun away from her, whistling for Rebel to follow.

Chapter Two

Kensie Morgan was trouble.

Colter watched her image shrink in his rearview mirror and tried to tell himself he'd done the right thing. The truth was, he longed to turn around and promise to help her, even though he really *wasn't* that kind of tracker. And neither was Rebel.

From the back seat, she let out a short howl, as if she disagreed with his choice to leave.

"She's no good for us, girl."

His conversation with Kensie felt like the longest sustained chat he'd had with anyone in a year. He knew it wasn't, but maybe she was just the first person he'd felt connected to in all that time. The first person he'd actually wanted to stay and talk to longer. And that was dangerous territory.

Cowardly or not, he was finished with human connection. He had Rebel; he had the sheer, uncomplicated beauty of Alaska. That was enough for him.

Rebel didn't mind the nightmares. She probably had them too, poor girl. And now that they'd both been cut loose from the service, she wasn't going to go and die on him anytime soon. As long as she stopped saving people's lives.

She nudged her head between the front seats, resting her chin on his arm as he maneuvered up the winding, unpaved road toward his cabin. It was up high, which made the trek tricky during the worst of winter, but the view was worth it.

Staring out over miles of nothing but snow-topped trees and breathing in the crisp, cold air, so unlike the deserts where he'd served, brought him as close to peace as he figured he'd ever get. And once a military man, always a military man. There was just something about having the high ground that helped him relax.

His closest neighbor was miles away, down in the valley. He rarely saw other vehicles on his ride out of town, and never in the last few miles. A vehicle coming up the final hill meant someone was coming to see him. And no one came to see him.

His parents still called him regularly, certain he had to be lonely. But they'd been afraid of the trip to Desparre, of the wild animals they were certain roamed everywhere and the thick, heavy winters that sometimes prevented travel in or out until spring came around again. They couldn't understand why he'd come here. But then, they'd never really understood him. Not when he'd joined the military right out of high school and not a decade later when he'd been forced to leave it.

They loved him, but they didn't realize what he'd been looking for or what he'd lost. Brotherhood. A bond he shared with no one but Rebel these days, because she'd been in the thick of it with him.

As he slowed the truck to a stop in front of his cabin, his breathing evened out. All the open space did that for him. Beside him, Rebel seemed to relax, too.

He opened the driver's side door, telling Rebel to stay as he hobbled around to the back. Normally she hopped into the front and climbed out after him, but he knew her injury almost as well as he knew his own. She might not be showing it, but she was in pain, too.

"Come on, girl," he urged, watching as she stepped gingerly to the ground. She led the way up to the cabin, favoring her back left leg.

"We'll sit by the fire and take it easy tonight," he promised her, earning a half-hearted tail wag.

As soon as he opened the door, she walked straight over and claimed a spot in front of the fireplace.

"Greedy," he teased her, and she gave him a look as if to say, *Get a move on. It's cold in here.*

He'd had the heat set too low, not expecting the cold to come so soon, although he should have been used to it. By the time he'd moved out here last October, the snow had been so high the real estate agent had needed his help clearing it away so they could even open the door.

He cranked the heat up now, then got to work building a fire. He poured Rebel some dog food and dragged it over to her. He was hungry, too, now that dinnertime was approaching, but his leg was more demanding than his stomach. So, instead of cooking, he settled in his recliner, gingerly lifting his right leg and wishing he'd grabbed some ice for it first. But now that he was settled, he didn't plan to move for a few hours.

Between the heater kicking on and the fireplace warming the cabin even more, Colter's stiff muscles slowly started to relax. An hour later, his leg was still throbbing unhappily, but the pain was a lot more manageable.

With the fire roaring away on one side of him, the view of the valley covered in snow through a thick-paned window on the other and Rebel at his side, Colter felt complete. This was why he'd come to Alaska. Yes, his parents' claim was true—he was hiding here. But he was hiding from all the well-meaning but clueless people—them included—who wanted to *fix* him. Who had no idea what it meant to survive an ambush when all of his brothers had died.

Rebel whimpered and when Colter glanced at her, he could swear she knew what he was thinking. "It's okay, girl."

But instead of calming down, she stood, went to the window and started barking.

Someone was here. And since there was no one in Alaska he knew well enough to visit his house, it wasn't a guest.

He'd come to Alaska to hide from what was left of his life. Yeah, he could admit that. But there were plenty of other people who saw Alaska as the final frontier: a place to hide away from something they'd done, to run from the law.

Colter winced as he swung his injured leg to the ground, then hobbled over to the cabinet against the far wall and grabbed his pistol. He'd stopped carrying it into town, but right now he was happy he hadn't given it up altogether.

"Rebel, quiet," he commanded. In her three years as a Military Working Dog, never once had she disobeyed a command from him.

But today she just barked louder.

Colter released the safety on his pistol and eased toward the door, preparing himself for trouble.

KENSIE GRIPPED THE steering wheel until her knuckles hurt, stomping her foot on the brake. But it didn't help. Her rental truck still slid backward, angling toward the edge of the road, toward the drop-off beside the steep hill she was trying to climb.

Why did Colter Hayes have to live in the middle of nowhere?

According to the few locals who would talk to her, he was an ex-Marine hiding from the world after being badly injured. No one seemed to know how he'd been injured or why exactly he wanted to hide. In fact, none of them seemed to know much more about him than the few details he'd shared with her on the street. And yet he'd lived in Desparre for almost a year.

"People come this far into the Alaskan wilderness for three reasons, honey," the grocery store owner had told her, then ticked off those reasons on gnarled fingers. "Either they love a good adventure, the kind that's as likely to get them killed as not. Or they want the entire world to leave them the heck alone. Or they've done something they don't want anyone to know about—probably something illegal—and they figure no one will ever track them down here."

Then she'd narrowed her eyes at Kensie. "We all assume Colter is the middle one. But you've got to be careful who you trust."

Her words echoed in Kensie's brain as her truck finally stopped its dangerous backward descent. She kept her foot wedged down hard on the brake, her hands locked tight on the wheel, afraid to move. Should she keep pushing forward or turn back?

She leaned forward, craning her head up at the hill in front of her. Snow was still falling on it, obscuring what was little more than a dirt trail.

She had one more crest to go and she wasn't sure if her truck would make it. But she wasn't sure she could turn it around, either.

Now it was her brother Flynn's voice she heard in her head. "You're going to *Alaska*, Kens? Are you crazy? People venture out into the woods there and never come out again. You could die up there and we'd never even know where to start looking."

At the time, she'd thought he was overreacting. He always had when it came to her, even now that they were both adults. He'd already lost his little sister and she knew, somewhere deep down that he'd never admit, he was afraid of losing his big sister, too.

She realized now how ill-prepared she'd been for this trip. Desparre was insular. People here already distrusted each other, but they distrusted her double for being an outsider. Some of them had been nice but ultimately dismissive. Others had just eyed her suspiciously and refused to talk. Questioning as many people in town as she could had told her that either no one knew anything about Alanna other than what they'd read in the news, or they just weren't going to tell her.

But Colter understood this place. And regardless of what he'd said about his tracking skills, she knew one thing. Trackers found people. Whether it was someone who'd set a bomb or someone who'd been kidnapped, she had to believe he could help her.

And she might not be prepared, but she was determined. If Alanna was really here, Kensie wasn't leaving without her.

Assuming she could get up this mountain.

Gritting her teeth, Kensie switched her foot from the brake to the gas as fast as she could, not wanting to lose traction. The truck's wheels spun, spraying snow at a crazy angle, and then it shot forward, up the hill.

Kensie grappled to keep control of the wheel, her muscles aching. The truck veered left, then right, but it kept moving upward until she could see the top of the hill. She was going to make it.

As if thinking those words had been bad luck, the truck veered right again, straight off the side of the road. It sank down several feet, jolting her forward as the front end planted itself in a snowbank.

Kensie swore, tears of frustration pricking her eyes. For fourteen years, leads on Alanna had come and gone like rabbits in a magician's disappearing act. One minute promising and solid and right in front of them. The next minute *poof!* Like they'd never even existed.

This time might be no different. Her family didn't think it was. But they'd come to accept years ago what statistics said was a near certainty: Alanna was gone. She was never coming home.

Kensie had never been able to do that. And she

didn't think it was guilt eating at her gut this time, telling her something was here. She had to believe that this time, if she looked hard enough, maybe the magic trick would become real.

Colter could help her. She knew he could. If she could find him. If she could convince him.

Was she even close to where he lived? She had no idea. She assumed she'd followed the directions properly, but what if there'd been a turnoff she'd missed? She could be miles from his cabin.

She peered through the windshield at the snowflakes, falling faster and thicker from the sky. It had been cold when she'd arrived, but temperatures had dropped to near zero in the hours since. And that was down in the main part of town, not up in the mountains where Colter lived.

Fear settled low in her belly as she zipped her coat up to her chin and slid her hood over her head, fastening it tightly. She didn't need to gun the engine to know there was no way she was getting her truck out of this snowbank.

She was walking from here. She just had to pray Colter's cabin was nearby and she wouldn't walk right by it in this snowstorm and then freeze to death.

Chapter Three

The moment she stepped out of the truck, Kensie wondered if she'd made a mistake. Her whole body seemed to ice over as her feet sank into a pile of snow, rising over the tops of her boots. The cold seeped through them, too, soaking her up to midcalf. She had to hold the tops of her boots to make sure they came with her as she climbed out of the snowbank and then her hands were soaked through her gloves.

Enormous snowflakes plopped on her head, sliding down the side of her hood, where some dropped off. The wind sent others flying into her face, where they left a watery trail down her neck and then slipped inside her coat.

She was going to die out here. She could already feel the icy cold in her lungs with every breath. What had she read about extreme cold bursting your lungs?

Calm down, she told herself. Colter's place had to be close. The grocery store owner had said the top of the final hill. There were no more hills to climb. And yet, no cabin.

There were a lot of trees, though, more than she'd expected this high up. She thought she could see a road marker ahead, leading a winding path through them. Colter's cabin could be behind the trees somewhere. But so could bears. Or she could get lost and not be able to find her way back to the truck. Every few steps, she glanced backward.

Soon she could no longer see the truck. Panic built inside her and she paused. Keep moving forward or turn back?

Then she heard it. Or maybe hypothermia had already started to set in and she was imagining the barking.

Kensie started to run. Her lungs protested every breath, painful from the cold, but as she rounded another copse of trees, there it was. A beautiful little cabin with a clear, perfect view of the valley below. She could even see a glacier from here. In other circumstances, she would have paused and soaked in the amazing vista.

Tears of relief spilled over and instantly froze on her cheeks and then Colter was there, his strong arm around her shoulders, leading her into his home.

She didn't even pause at the doorway, wondering if it was really a good idea to trust a man she'd just met. She simply let him help her inside.

As soon as she was through the doorway, Rebel

pressed up against her side. The dog stayed with her until Colter pushed her into a big recliner near the fire. Then Rebel sat primly next to her, soft brown eyes full of worry.

The heat from the fireplace made Kensie shiver. It didn't make any sense, but she couldn't seem to stop as Colter bent down with a pained grunt. He pulled the sopping wet boots from her feet and propped her legs up near the fireplace. Then he peeled the gloves from her hands, rubbing them between his own big, calloused palms until the warmth finally penetrated.

And so did his words. "What are you doing here? Wandering around in this weather is dangerous. Do you have some kind of death wish?"

Before she could bristle, he let out a heavy sigh and stopped rubbing her hands. "Hold them by the fire. I'll make you some cocoa."

"My truck hit a snowbank," she managed through chattering teeth.

"But why were you up here to begin with?" he asked, looking like he wasn't sure he wanted to know the answer as he walked into the connecting kitchen.

"I came to see you. I need your help. No one here will talk to me. But you know them. You know the area. You know how to track—"

"I told you, Kensie, Rebel and I don't do that anymore. And the kind of tracking you're talking about, we never did. It's not the same thing. Dogs are trained to do one thing. You can't just switch them over, make a drug-sniffing dog an explosives one. Doesn't work like that. And finding people without a direct trail? Even if we had a scent to work from, we wouldn't be able to do that."

Kensie felt her shoulders drop. She'd come all this way. This couldn't be the end of it.

Colter kept talking as he put a pot on the little stove and poured in milk and cocoa. She barely heard his words as she thought about the note that had been found. Thought about Alanna, somewhere in the Alaskan wilderness with her kidnapper.

"…Military Police don't do that. In a war zone—"

Kensie's head snapped up. "What did you say?"

"That kind of tracking work," Colter said, as the scent of cocoa filled Kensie's nostrils. "We don't—"

"No, not that. You said you were Military Police?"

"Yeah." The word was full of wariness.

"So, you know how to run an investigation."

"So do the civilian police. And they actually have authority here," Colter said as he handed her a steaming mug of cocoa.

The heat felt wonderful in her hands, the scent tempting her. But she just clutched it and stared up at him. "They don't want to help me."

He frowned as he lowered himself stiffly onto the chair on the other side of the fireplace. "Why not?"

Internally, she cursed her stupidity. If he knew the truth about what the FBI thought, he'd call her crazy, too. He'd probably join the chorus of people trying to get her to return home.

She postponed answering him by taking a gulp of the cocoa. It burned its way down her throat, making her eyes water, but it also seemed to warm her from the inside, so she took another sip and then another. When the mug was almost empty, she lowered it to her lap, realizing her teeth had finally stopped chattering.

Pins and needles danced along her feet and hands, but they'd gone numb when she'd been outside. The painful return of sensation was a good thing.

"Kensie," Colter prompted, staring at her with light blue eyes fringed with pale brown lashes.

He was more than just good-looking. The hard, battle-worn expression he seemed to constantly wear disguised it, but when he stared at her like he was now—with curiosity and sympathy—awareness settled low in her belly.

Suddenly, it wasn't just the scent of cocoa tempting her.

His dark blond hair was cropped close, military style, but she suspected it would be soft if she ran her hands through it. There was no hint of matching scruff on the hard planes of his jaw, but she wanted to slide her hands over the skin there, too, to pull him close and see how much control he'd have if she kissed him.

As she stared, his pupils dilated. Fire seemed to race over the icy surface of her cheeks and she ducked her head, trying to gain control of her emotions.

It had to be the fear of dying all alone of hypothermia. Or the stress of chasing after Alanna. Or maybe she'd just ignored her own needs for too long.

"It's old," Kensie blurted, hoping he hadn't noticed what she realized had been blatant ogling. But of course he had, or she wouldn't have seen the reciprocal attraction.

"What's old?"

She wanted to smile at the confusion in his voice, a little part of her hoping he was still as distracted as she was. The more sensible side of her brain reminded her that she was stranded in his cabin and she barely knew the man.

The voice of reason in her mind won. She straightened in her seat, meeting his gaze with an all-business stare. "The case is fourteen years cold." She shrugged, hoping he'd believe it, because it was the truth. It just wasn't the whole truth.

She rubbed Rebel's chin with her free hand, to distract herself from the lie by omission. She prayed he wouldn't read it on her face.

"So, they're not going to help you?" He sounded incredulous and a little outraged.

The combination just made her like him more. But she couldn't afford to be distracted by him. Not when Alanna might be out there somewhere. Not when everything inside of her was screaming that he could be the break she'd been waiting for most of her life.

And she had him. She could feel it. He sympathized with her pain and he had skills she'd never possess. With his help, they might really be able to bring Alanna home.

"It's a resources thing." She paraphrased what she'd been told hundreds of times over the years. Police always had to work on new cases, missing persons who hadn't been gone for years, who had a higher chance of rescue. The longer someone was missing, the less chance they had of ever being found.

Years ago, they'd first learned the realities about Alanna coming home as months went by with less and less interest from the police and the community. Her parents had made a promise. They'd do whatever it took to be sure that wasn't Alanna's fate.

But fourteen years of disappointment and two other children who needed them had taken its toll. Kensie knew it was her turn to take up the torch and keep that promise.

She stared expectantly at Colter, sensing his

next words would be a wary agreement to try and help.

But he just shook his head sadly. "Believe me, I understand your pain, Kensie. Probably better than you realize. But I'm no good for you. I'm no good for anyone. I can't help you."

MAYBE SHE *WAS* CRAZY.

It wasn't just her parents and Flynn who'd begged her not to fly out to Alaska on a questionable piece of evidence and a thin thread of hope. It was also her friends, the ones who'd been by her side since childhood, who'd watched how the constant surge of hope followed by inevitable, bitter disappointment had almost torn them all apart.

She'd overheard family friends talking about how Flynn's car accident had been a necessary wake-up call for her parents, reminding them they still had two children who needed them. And in some ways, it had. But it had also been the day they'd decided to accept something Kensie never would: that Alanna was gone for good.

But right now, hopelessness reared up.

After his announcement that he wouldn't help her, Colter had gone outside to dig out her truck over her objections. The whole time he'd been gone, she was worried he'd hurt his leg or freeze out there. But he'd bundled up in much better winter gear than she owned and forty-five minutes later, he'd reappeared.

She could tell he was trying to hide how badly his leg hurt, so she'd forced herself to keep quiet rather than asking. But guilt had followed her closely as Colter drove behind her rental all the way back into town. She'd parked by the police station where she'd first seen him playing fetch with Rebel, rolled down her window and debated what to say. She'd known him only a few hours and yet she'd been struggling to say goodbye.

Apparently, he had no such quandary. He'd given her a wave, a solemn "Good luck," and off he and Rebel had gone.

She'd probably never see them again.

The idea left a bad taste in her mouth.

But right now, she had to figure out how to move forward. She'd come here alone, with no expectation of help from an ex-Marine with investigative and tracking experience. Nothing had changed. She could still do this alone.

As many times as she told herself that, she still felt Colter's absence like a huge blow to her goal of finding Alanna. And maybe a little bit of a personal blow, too, although she didn't know him well enough to feel anything more than unsatisfied lust.

"Get over it," Kensie muttered. If Colter wouldn't help her, she'd do it herself.

After her experience slamming into that snowbank up near Colter's cabin, her first stop should have been to get better winter gear. But down in the main part of town, the snow was slowing and the accumulation was much less. Only an inch or two of slushy white coated the streets.

More than a pair of warm boots, Kensie needed a mental boost. Something had to go right, something to reassure her that she wasn't chasing a ghost. Maybe there would be a lead at the store where the note had been found. If she could locate the store itself.

Having an immediate goal made Kensie feel better. She steeled herself as she stepped out of her rental and back into the cold, but couldn't stop the shiver that raced up her spine. As quickly as possible, she stomped back into the grocery store where the woman had helped her before.

The instant Kensie walked inside, the woman—who was probably the owner as well as the cashier—looked up. Her steel-gray eyes, the same shade as her long braid, were sharp and knowing. "He was no help?"

Kensie shrugged in response, not wanting to badmouth Colter after he'd whipped her up a pot of cocoa, warmed her hands between his own and dug her truck out of the snow despite a badly injured leg. "It was a silly idea," she said instead.

The woman let out a grunt that sounded like she disagreed. "What else do you need?"

A small smile tugged at Kensie's lips. Living in a place like this must teach you to read people. As the bell dinged behind her, announcing another customer, Kensie said, "Colter Hayes has his own troubles. But I still need to find the store where the note was found. Do you think you could draw me a map? The roads are really confusing out here."

"That's because our roads are what you city folk would call hiking trails. Honey, you might want to wait until the snow clears. It's out on the edge of town—so far out, most people don't even think of it as part of Desparre. Owned by a cranky old guy who's as likely to close for the day as not if the mood strikes."

Ignoring the little voice in her head reminding her what had happened when she insisted on driving to Colter's place in this weather, Kensie shook her head. "I want to try today. I need some good news right now."

"He might not have any."

"I know," Kensie said over the lump that had risen in her throat. She swallowed the discomfort back. She had to stay positive.

If she didn't keep searching for her sister, who would?

"All right," the woman agreed with a deep frown that told Kensie she didn't approve. But she drew a map and explained it three times.

Kensie thanked her, then headed back into the cold. She eyed the clothing store down the street, wondering if they'd have better winter gear, then looked up. The sun was hanging low, casting beautiful shades of red and orange across the sky.

If she wanted to talk to the owner and get back to her hotel before it got dark, she needed to go now.

A tap on her shoulder made Kensie jump.

The man standing there backed up a step as she turned to face him. "Sorry, I didn't mean to startle you."

He was almost as tall and muscular as Colter. Almost as good-looking too, with jet-black hair and chocolate-brown eyes. Kensie lowered her arms.

"I heard you talking to Talise." She must have looked perplexed, because he added, "In the grocery store. You're looking for Jasper's General Store?"

Kensie nodded, clutching the hand-drawn map she still wasn't completely certain she could follow.

"I can take you if you want. My truck's right over there." He pointed to a massive vehicle parked in front of hers.

It was probably much more solid in the snow than her rental, but what did she know about this guy? Back home, she'd never get into a truck with a stranger. Of course, back home, she never would have driven out to a stranger's cabin, either.

Because even though a little voice in her head kept insisting she and Colter had a connection, the reality was that she didn't know him.

As if reading her thoughts, the guy stuck out his hand. "I'm Danny Weston. Former military just like your friend Colter." He gave her a big, crooked, boyish-looking grin. "Although Colter was Marines. I was Air Force. Grunts versus high flyers. Just kidding," he added as she took his hand.

It closed loosely around her own, as if he was afraid to hurt her as he shook. Then he gave her a firm shake anyway. Must have been a military thing.

Kensie had an internal debate. She didn't know Danny, but she didn't know Colter, either. And that had turned out fine. Besides, this was about her sister. *If it wasn't for me, Alanna never would have been kidnapped.* Kensie nodded to Danny. "Yeah, that would be great. Thank you."

"Sure." He led her over to the massive vehicle and held open the passenger door. "We can talk to old Jasper and then I'll have you back here in an hour, before it gets dark."

The last of her doubts fled as she settled into the comfortable passenger seat. "That sounds perfect."

Danny smiled at her again, then slammed the door shut and ran around to the driver's side. He started up the engine and was just stretching his seatbelt across his lap when the driver's door was ripped open and he went flying out of the truck.

Surprise and panic shot through her as Kensie's gaze darted to the perpetrator. Colter.

"Get out of the truck now!" Colter yelled at her,

his voice deep and commanding. Rebel stood beside and slightly behind him, teeth bared.

The panic intensified. She fumbled with her seatbelt as Danny climbed to his feet. She tried to open the door, but there was no door handle on the inside, just an empty space where it should have been.

Kensie shoved at the door, but nothing happened. She launched herself across the bench seat, straight toward Danny.

He was squaring off, facing Colter, as though he was about to take a swing. But across the street, people were starting to come out of businesses, maybe because they'd heard Colter's yell.

Danny paused, and while she still could, Kensie shoved herself out of the truck. Her body brushed past him and he started to turn toward her.

Her heart was pounding out of control, her limbs heavy and awkward in her fear. Then Colter's hand closed around hers, pulling her first to him and then shoving her behind him. The fear shifted, no longer for her own safety.

Two men who'd come out of the hardware store were slowly walking their way. Talise stood outside with a cell phone to her ear and her eyes on the police station down the road.

She knew Colter was strong from the way he'd practically lifted her off her feet just now, but with his bad leg, would Danny hurt him? Kensie's whole body began to shake as she glanced back toward the police station, willing officers to come outside.

"Drive away while you still can," Colter said in a low, menacing tone that sent shivers up her arms.

Rebel crouched low on her haunches and took a slow step forward, growling deep in her throat.

Danny took one last glance at the approaching townspeople, then gave Rebel a nervous look. He let out a string of nasty curses directed at Colter. Then he jumped in the truck and pulled away so fast she and Colter had to leap backward to avoid being hit.

As soon as Danny was gone, Colter spun toward her. The fury on his face was unlike anything she'd ever seen. His jaw was hard, his lips turned out in a near snarl. His eyes were narrowed into furious slits. But he took a deep breath and the tension disappeared, his face smoothing back into what seemed to be his default—not happy and mild, but serious and steady.

Next to him, Rebel straightened, then sat, as if nothing had happened.

"I'll help you," he told her.

"What?" She was almost more shocked than when he'd pulled Danny out of his truck.

"On one condition."

"Okay."

"It's just me, Kensie. You don't get into some random jerk's truck. That guy—" He broke off, blowing out a breath, then finished. "*I* help you and no one else."

The fear that had filled her a moment ago drained away, leaving her exhausted. But a smile built up inside. This was what she needed. This was *who* she needed. Colter was her best chance to change everything that hurt in her life.

He held out a hand. "We have a deal?"

Kensie placed her hand in his, liking the way his fingers closed solidly over hers, as if he knew she was strong enough not to be crushed. "Deal."

Chapter Four

Danny Weston had nearly kicked his ass.

Colter shoved down the embarrassment and tried to be thankful for the show of support from the townspeople. Despite the fact that he'd been here almost a year, the people of Desparre barely knew him. But they probably knew Danny. And what they knew, he was pretty sure they didn't like.

On a good day, Colter could take a guy like Danny down with ease. But it had been a long time since he'd had a good day. He knew his limitations and, right now, his leg was screaming at him.

It was a small price compared to the one his brothers had paid, but it stung to be so useless in a situation he should have been able to handle himself. Some badass Staff Sergeant he was.

Of course, he wasn't a military man at all anymore, except in his mind.

Turning around and heading back into town after he'd dropped Kensie off had been a fluke.

A nagging sense that he'd regret it if he didn't help her look for her sister, even if he had no idea where to start.

He glanced at her now, absently petting Rebel from the seat beside him. Her lips were clenched in a tight line and her head was bowed slightly, as though Desparre was beating her. She'd barely said a word since she'd followed him back to his truck, but she'd done a poor job of hiding her shaking.

Anger at Danny for making her feel that way overtook his embarrassment, but even that was quickly eclipsed by fear. Fear over what could have happened if she'd ridden off in Danny's truck instead of his.

And nothing had been done about it. Police had shown up and taken his statement—and Kensie's, about the missing door handle inside Danny's truck. But the officers had shaken their heads, telling Colter he was lucky Danny wasn't pressing charges for assault. When Colter argued about the door handle—obviously meant to keep someone trapped—they'd said it wasn't a crime to have a broken truck.

As someone who'd run investigations himself, Colter understood their dilemma. But that same experience told him Danny was still a threat.

He shot another glance Kensie's way, unable to stop himself from drinking in a quick look at her. Reassuring himself she was safe.

Catching his look, she said softly, "Danny said he was Air Force. I thought I could trust him."

"I really am a Marine," Colter blurted.

Thankfully, she looked more perplexed than startled by his outburst.

"An MP. Military Police," he clarified. "I served for almost a decade, rose to the rank of Staff Sergeant. I doubt Danny Weston's gotten any closer to the service than walking past a recruiting booth."

"I shouldn't have believed him."

Her voice was so low he almost didn't catch it. His hands tightened on the wheel of his truck as he continued his slow, steady drive along one of Desparre's back roads out of town. "The guy's a creep, but he's smart. Good at getting people to trust him. Especially women."

"I think he was in the grocery store. He heard me talking about you. It seemed like he knew you."

"Yeah, he knows me. But we're not friends." Colter and Danny had crossed paths a few times since he'd moved to Desparre. Once had been in the bar where Danny was trying a little too hard to get a local woman to go home with him. Colter had walked her to her car, but he suspected if there hadn't been people watching, Danny would have come at him that night. A few times since, Colter had seen him around, and the guy had set his radar off.

He had no idea what had brought Danny to

Desparre, but he suspected it wasn't good. And he didn't trust the guy within a mile of Kensie.

"Just steer clear of him, Kensie."

"Yeah, I got it."

There was an edge to her voice that he suspected came as much from fear as it did from anger.

He drew in a deep breath through his nose, trying to calm his emotions. Yeah, it hadn't been smart of her to get into a stranger's truck, but how mad could he be when he'd essentially asked her to do the same thing with him?

She didn't know him. She was acting on blind faith and desperation. They were feelings he knew well. As much as he didn't want to get involved in anything remotely resembling a mission, he couldn't let that desperation lead her into danger again.

Because if Alanna had been grabbed by a guy like Danny, it was probably already too late to save her.

The errant thought left a bitter taste in his mouth and he shoved back the inevitable memories that followed, of the last moments he'd seen the brothers he'd loved. Brothers he would have traded his own life for if he could have.

He prayed Kensie wouldn't have to live with the same grief.

"So, the store," he said, trying to clear the fog that always threatened whenever he thought about that day, his last day in the military. "Tell me what you know."

She glanced his way, her beautiful eyes clearing, like this was the distraction she needed, too. "Not much. Apparently the owner found it in a stack of money. The chief of police told me Jasper didn't know who'd left it there, but I'm thinking we can ask him about everyone who came in that day. Or maybe he'll recognize me. My sister might still resemble me."

Her last words were full of hope and wistfulness, and he tried to remember how cold she'd told him the case was. "You said she disappeared fourteen years ago?"

"Yeah. She'd be nineteen now."

"How old were you when—"

"When she was kidnapped?" Kensie finished. "I was thirteen."

She didn't offer any more, so Colter let the silence remain, let Rebel take up the task of relaxing Kensie. His dog seemed more than up for it, leaning between the seats and practically hanging her head in Kensie's lap.

"I think she likes me," Kensie said, amusement in her tone.

"Yeah, she transitioned better into civilian life than I did. I think she'd be friends with everyone if she could."

It wasn't totally true. Like most dogs, she seemed to have an innate sense of who she could trust. But she definitely would like it if he'd let more people into his life, give her someone else to spoil her.

Kensie laughed as Rebel nuzzled even closer, her front feet practically in the seat with them now. "Well, thanks for making an exception and being my friend."

Was that what he'd done? He let the idea rattle around in his brain as they pulled up to the store out in a little strip of shops off the beaten path. Yeah, he guessed it was. He'd saved her life, she'd seen his home, and he cared about what happened to her. Plus, he sympathized over what happened to her sister. A year after leaving the military, he'd made his first new friend. As much as he liked Kensie, it left him unsettled.

"Let's go see what we can get out of Jasper." As he spoke the words, a familiar determination filled him, one he'd prayed wouldn't return. The feeling of a mission.

Instantly, his chest tightened and breathing seemed more difficult. The doctors at the VA hospital had told him the PTSD might always be with him. Sometimes it would be flashbacks, other times panic attacks or nightmares. They said he needed to learn to recognize the triggers and manage his response. But that was easier said than done.

Rebel's head swung toward him, her ears twitching. The first few months after he'd gotten out, there were times when something as simple as a branch snapping would send him right back onto that battlefield and the first crack of the sniper rifle. And he wasn't the only one; more than once, he'd found Rebel cowering in the bathtub during a thunderstorm. Or she'd leap on him, trying to protect him from a car backfiring, and re-aggravate both of their injuries.

Rebel knew exactly what was happening right now. But he didn't want Kensie to see his weakness, so he flung open the truck door and practically fell out of it.

The cold air shocked his system, filling his lungs and stopping the spasms in his chest. He clenched and unclenched his fists, a trick he'd learned at the hospital accidentally. It helped ground him, give him control over one small thing.

By the time Rebel leaped to the ground beside him and Kensie hurried around the truck, he felt back in control.

She squinted at him. "You okay?"

"Yeah. Let's do this." It was something he'd always say to Rebel when they were about to track a scent. It came out now without thought, but instead of provoking another attack, it straightened his shoulders and filled him with strength.

Beside him, Rebel seemed to strain forward, even though she was always off leash. She sensed a new mission as much as he did. Unlike him, she seemed truly ready.

Thank goodness her injury hadn't fully healed.

The selfish thought hit unexpectedly. But if Rebel had healed while he hadn't, she would have been back at war, assigned to a new soldier. The only reason he'd gotten to keep her was that the huge piece of metal that had gone straight through his leg had also pierced her. Neither of them would ever be a hundred percent whole again. Which meant the military didn't want them anymore.

"Okay," Kensie said, obviously not realizing the dark place where his thoughts had traveled. She strode up the snowy walkway toward the store.

He followed, trying not to be distracted by the subtle sway of her hips under her parka. Rebel trotted along beside him, ready for the kind of action she'd been trained to handle.

As soon as they walked through the door, a bell dinged and Jasper Starn glared their way. With his chrome-silver hair slicked back on his head and his dark skin over-weathered by the Alaskan wind, he could have been anywhere between sixty and a hundred. He'd lived somewhere on the outskirts of Desparre and run this store for as long as anyone in town seemed to remember. And he was possibly the crankiest store owner Colter had ever met.

When they approached him instead of walking around the store, Jasper looked them up and down like he was cataloguing places they might be hiding weapons, then grunted.

Seemingly not put off by the less than cordial welcome, Kensie gave him a wide smile. It didn't seem to do much for Jasper's mood, but dang if it didn't make Colter feel a little lighter.

"I'm Kensie Morgan."

His lips pursed, but he made no other sign he'd heard her.

Kensie's smile faltered a little. "I'm Alanna Morgan's sister. I know you found the note—"

"I got nothing to say about that." Jasper cut her off, then angled his glare toward Colter. "No pets in the store. I've told you that before."

Colter nodded at Rebel, who promptly sat. At sixty-five pounds of pure, lean muscle, and always at attention, she could be intimidating. "We just have a few questions. The quicker you answer them, the quicker we're all out of here."

"I already talked to the FBI and the police. You want to know about it, ask them."

Kensie's smile dropped off. Probably she was used to people being accommodating—or at least polite—when she asked them about her missing sister.

Colter took an aggressive step forward, slamming his hand down on the counter. Sensing his mood, Rebel came up next to him, baring her teeth a little.

Then Kensie's hand landed on top of his. It

was soft and slender and unexpected and it totally threw him off his game.

"I was there the day she went missing," Kensie said, her voice a pained whisper that made even Jasper freeze. "I was thirteen. I was supposed to be watching her, but I was reading a book up by the house while she ran around the front yard."

A sudden, wistful smile broke across her face. "Alanna was five. She was wearing this blue flowered dress, covered in dirt because she liked to play with everything. She was so grubby—her hands, her face—but the cutest little kid. She had these dimples you wouldn't even know were there until she grinned, and then this sparkle in her eyes that told you she was about to be trouble."

Kensie took a deep breath and Colter felt the shaking through her hand. He flipped his over and closed it around her palm, trying to give her support even as his mind warned him he was treading in dangerous territory. Connection.

Kensie's fingers spasmed slightly in his, but that was the only sign she'd noticed. Her gaze was laser locked on Jasper. "I saw the car pull up. I saw the guy grab Alanna." Her voice broke. "I dropped my stupid book and ran after them, but they sped away. It was the last time I ever saw her."

Colter had been in Jasper's store more than a dozen times since he'd moved to Desparre. For the first time, he saw the man twitch and his glare soften.

"Look, I'm not playing games here," Jasper said, his tone conciliatory. "I found the note stuck in a stack of money in my cash drawer at the end of the day two weeks ago. I don't know how it got there."

"Okay," Kensie said, leaning forward. "Do you remember any of the people who came in the store that day? Maybe a young woman—about nineteen—who looked like me?"

Jasper's lips twisted as he stared at Kensie. "Maybe. Someone with dark hair like yours did come in that day, but she was with her family. I don't know who she was. Hadn't seen her before and haven't seen her since."

Jasper's was a regular stop for people who really lived off the beaten path. So if Jasper had only seen the girl once—if it was even Alanna—she might have just been passing through.

Kensie's shoulders dropped and her gaze sought his, as if she was looking for him to find a new path forward. But he wasn't sure there was one.

If Alanna had been in the store on her way to some even more remote part of Alaska, how would they ever trace her?

Colter knew what it was like to live with a desperate, burning hope, as painful as it was powerful. But he also knew that sometimes there was relief in release, too. He'd never return to the person he'd been before he lost his brothers. But when he'd woken in the hospital and no one would tell him if his brothers were okay, he'd been frozen. Sometimes he wished he could return to that state of hopeful ignorance, but it meant being stuck, unable to move forward at all.

Finding Alanna might be impossible. If it was, what if Kensie was frozen forever?

"WE NEED TO talk to the police."

Colter leveled his best Marine stare at Kensie across the table in the tiny restaurant off the main strip in Desparre. He'd pulled in on a whim because she'd looked so defeated after talking to Jasper that he hadn't just wanted to drop her at her truck all alone. And if he was being honest, he didn't want to say goodbye quite yet.

Because it was a place he came semiregularly and because Desparre was usually low-key, they let Rebel sit beside the booth as he and Kensie quietly sipped coffee. Her eyes were downcast, maybe to avoid his stare. But then, it hadn't worked on her the first four times he'd suggested this course of action.

"What's your hesitation? I know you talked to them once, but they're not going to spill everything they know just because Alanna is your sister. If we go in and ask pointed questions about the note, we might get somewhere."

"Yeah, maybe."

He frowned, trying to figure out if talking to Jasper had discouraged her as much as it had him or if something else was going on. "It's worth a shot, right?" he pressed, surprised with himself for playing cheerleader. He'd known this woman less than a day and already he'd spent more time with her than anyone else since his doctors at the VA hospital. Not only that, he was actually pushing her to press forward, when he'd been the one who'd wanted out in the first place.

Truth be told, he still wanted out. The last thing he needed was a mission. But Kensie had a pull about her he couldn't deny.

She took a heavy breath before meeting his gaze. "You're right."

"Okay, then," he said, forcing himself to sound more cheerful than he felt and praying he wasn't just giving her false hope. "Let's do this."

At his words, Rebel's head popped up and a grin tugged his lips. This time, instead of leading him down memory lane toward a panic attack, the idea of having a mission just made him feel wistful. If only it happened like that more often. But although he'd gotten better at avoiding triggers, it wasn't the same thing that set him off every time.

"We're not working, girl," he told Rebel, who yawned and settled down on her tummy.

Kensie gave him an incredulous stare. "She understands you, doesn't she?"

His smile grew a little. "You've never had a pet, huh? Trust me, they understand way more than you'd think."

She shook her head. "Nah, we lived in the city until I was ten, then my parents finally decided three kids in a walk-up was too much and moved out to the suburbs. By then I'd kind of given up asking for a pet. I thought Alanna was going to be the one to wear them down about getting a dog. After she was gone, none of us had time for things like that."

Things like what? A childhood? He studied her, trying to imagine what her life had been like after her sister had gone missing. Trying to imagine the guilt she'd internalized at such a young age when it clearly hadn't been her fault.

He knew all about that. He understood how irrational survivor's guilt could be, just like he understood that knowing it didn't make it go away. But he'd been an adult, faced with an inevitable consequence of war. She'd been just a child. And yet, until she'd spoken those words to Jasper, he never would have suspected she blamed herself.

He barely knew her, but she came across as competent and positive. He supposed it showed that the front you put on for others didn't always match what was underneath.

He dropped some money on the table for their coffees and stood, trying not to cringe as his leg spasmed. They needed to do this before the police station closed.

Desparre wasn't big enough to warrant twenty-four-hour coverage. Officers here were on call after a certain hour, but the station would be closed. He checked his watch—8:00 p.m. They had one hour and then they'd be out of luck.

Kensie stood more slowly, taking one last, long gulp of coffee as if she was either preparing herself for something or delaying moving forward. Rebel followed Kensie's lead—probably her leg was hurting, too.

Twenty minutes later they were back in town. Desparre had a few old streetlamps casting dim light over the main road, but otherwise it had grown dark while they'd been inside the coffee shop. The place looked like a ghost town, except for the light and rock music spilling out of the bar.

Kensie got out of the truck first, moving quickly. Rebel trotted by her side, only a hint of her injury showing in the way she favored her back left leg.

Colter grasped the door hard and lowered himself out slowly. Sitting in the car and then the coffee shop had stiffened up his leg. Without giving it enough time elevated, the muscle above his knee felt knotted into an immobile mess.

He forced it to move, gritting his teeth as he tried not to limp, just in case Kensie looked back. The military had drilled into him that failure and weakness weren't options. He'd already failed, but he had no intention of looking weak in front of her. Not again.

Ahead of him, Kensie reached for the door to

the police station, then jumped back as it opened from inside. Next to her, Rebel looked back to him, as if debating whether he needed her more than Kensie did.

She'd never taken to another human the way she had to Kensie. Not since he and Rebel had bonded on the battlefield had she so readily accepted anyone. Then again, he hadn't given her a lot of chances to spend time with civilians, outside his parents and the doctors at the various hospitals.

Apparently deciding he was fine, Rebel turned back to Kensie, who was now standing face-to-face with Chief Hernandez. She was bundled up, obviously heading out for the night, and she looked less than happy to see Kensie.

Colter picked up his pace, biting down against the pain. He'd be paying for this later, but he'd seen too many veterans get hooked on painkillers or booze after life-altering injuries. So he stayed away from all of it and just took the pain. Maybe it was his penance for living when everyone else had died.

"Miss Morgan, there's not much more we can tell you about your sister." Chief Hernandez nodded at him as he pushed his way up beside Kensie. "Colter."

"Chief. What about the girl who came into the store the day the note was found?"

"What girl?"

"The one who looked kind of like Kensie. She was there at the same time as a family."

The chief gave a tight smile. "You mean the one there *with* her family? We don't know who that was, but we did talk to Jasper about what he remembered. And that was a family, not a scared girl trying to escape."

She looked at Kensie, who'd shrunk low into her oversized parka. "I'm sorry. I wish we could help."

When she started to walk away, Colter blocked her. "What's the problem? Is the case still open?" He heard the confrontational note in his voice, but couldn't stop it.

She frowned and shoved her hands in the pockets of her parka. "Technically, we let the FBI take over. We checked it out. There's nothing more we can do." She looked at Kensie. "I'm sorry. I understand this is hard to hear, but—"

"Hard to hear? What? That the police won't do their job?" Colter tried to keep the words inside. But either he'd lost his social skills during his self-imposed hideout this past year or he was just in military mode, assuming everyone was an enemy until proven otherwise.

He swore internally, but before he could figure out how to backtrack, Chief Hernandez stepped toward him, getting in his space.

Rebel bared her teeth and even Kensie sidled closer to him in a silent show of support, but the chief sounded more tired than mad when she finally spoke.

"We did our job. I think you're low on information, Colter. We worked closely with the FBI on this. It was their call in the end, but we agreed with them."

She looked briefly at Kensie, then focused her attention on him again. "Kensie already knows this because the FBI told her, but let me share what they determined after running down all the leads: The note was a hoax."

Chapter Five

He'd spent the entire day battling his re-injured leg and fighting the flashbacks of losing the people he'd loved most in the world. And the whole time, she'd been lying to him?

Colter bit back all the things he wanted to say to Kensie as Chief Hernandez walked away. *Get control of your emotions*, he ordered himself. But still, the anger and frustration bubbled up. He'd taken on a mission for her. All for a lead that had already been ruled a hoax.

"Colter, before you say anything…" Kensie put a hand on his bicep.

An hour ago, he would have leaned into her touch, however small. Now, his arm flexed instinctively, like a shove to push her away.

She must have felt it, because she withdrew her hand and used it to stroke Rebel's fur instead. His dog tilted her head up, looking for more, and Colter couldn't help his frown.

"I know why you feel like I misled you—"

"Because you did?"

She huffed out a breath. "Yes, I did. But I wouldn't be here if I believed the FBI. I flew 3,500 miles for this. I know it's real this time."

His anger melted a little at the quiver in her voice. She was on a fool's mission. She probably knew it, too, but couldn't admit it to herself any more than she could to anyone else.

Maybe reason would help her get there. "Why does the FBI think it's a hoax?" He'd intended the question to be conversational, but it came out confrontational.

He really did need to work on his social skills. Before his accident, he'd had no problem relating to people. Apparently a year without practice was all it took to reduce him to a Neanderthal.

"The note said, *My name is Alanna Morgan, from Chicago. I'm still alive. I'm not the only one*."

She said the words as if she'd more than memorized them. As if she'd internalized them. As if they were a direct link to the sister she hadn't seen in fourteen years.

"Okay," he said when she didn't continue.

"We didn't live in Chicago anymore. We lived in the suburbs. We'd moved there when Alanna was three, and Alanna knew her address. The FBI thinks someone just picked the details from a news story, because reporters usually simplified it to Chicago."

"What makes you think that's not what happened?"

"Who would do that, all these years later, so

far away?" Her voice was plaintive, desperation seeping through, and he understood.

It wasn't so much that she knew it wasn't a hoax. She just couldn't bear it.

"Kensie—"

"I know what you're thinking. You're right, okay? There have been so many false leads over the years. This can't be another one. It just can't. But there's more to it than that. I feel it deep down in a way I can't quite explain. There's something here. I know there is. And the FBI had their chance; I thought they'd come up with something. When they didn't, I knew I had to come myself."

"The FBI has a lot of experience—"

Her hand stroked Rebel's head more frantically. "The FBI didn't know my sister."

"So they can probably be more objective about this. Look." He cut her off as she started to speak again. "Why would your sister say she wasn't the only one? That sounds like someone looking for attention, not a real letter. If this were real, why wouldn't your sister provide some detail to prove it was her?"

"She was five when she went missing, Colter. How much does she even remember about us? What would she say?"

Kensie sounded defeated, but then she took a deep breath and pressed on. "For years, my parents spent all their time doing everything they could to try and find Alanna. She was the baby.

We couldn't function properly as a family without her. And then my brother Flynn turned sixteen. I was twenty and Alanna had been gone for seven years, but my parents hadn't given up. I tried to watch out for Flynn better than I'd done for Alanna, but he got into a lot of trouble. He crashed the car, almost died. And it changed everything."

Colter sighed, knowing what Kensie was doing. The same thing she'd done with Jasper by telling the store owner personal details about the day her sister went missing. Playing on his sympathies to get him to continue helping her.

But as much as he sympathized with what she'd been through, dragging herself through a pointless search and him through the hell of a new mission wouldn't do either of them any good.

"I'm sorry for what you and your family have been through, Kensie, but—"

"We all worked so hard to stay close, to be good to each other, but sometimes I feel like we're just playing roles. That none of us has really been the same since Alanna went missing and we'll never be until we find her."

"Maybe you need to look for a new normal."

"Like you have?" Her hand lifted from Rebel's head and she crossed both arms over her chest.

"Yeah," he snapped back. "Maybe it's not perfect, but it works for me."

"It *works* for you? All alone up in that cabin, locking out the world?"

Rebel whimpered, nudging Kensie's thigh with her head, but Kensie ignored her this time.

"You don't know anything about my life, Kensie."

"And you don't know anything about mine! You don't know what it's like to lose your little sister, to watch her be taken right in front of you."

He clamped his jaw shut, trying to keep his words at bay, but they poured out anyway. "I know more about loss and grief than you can possibly understand. You come here and insist I help you, but at the end of the day, you're selfish. You're hiding the truth from me, wasting my time as much as your own. Are you really thinking about your sister, or is this about you, about making up for a stupid mistake you made at thirteen years old?"

He regretted the words as soon as they were out of his mouth and he tried to backtrack. "It wasn't your fault. But this mission you're on is about *you*."

Her lips curled up. "Right, and everything you do is for someone else? I don't know what happened to your leg, Colter, and I'm sorry that you can't be a soldier anymore, but maybe you should get over it! All I'm asking is for you to do something you're already good at. All I need is a little help. The FBI is wrong. I *know* they are."

His leg twitched at her reminder. Rebel whined again and left Kensie's side, pressing against him as if to hold him up. He could tell her what had happened to his unit, about just how well he understood not wanting to let someone go when deep down you knew you had to. But he held the words in. They'd only make her feel bad and they wouldn't do him any good, either. He wasn't even sure he could talk about it.

Instead, he shook his head sadly. "I hope you're right, Kensie, but I don't think you are. And I can't follow you on a fool's mission. I'm sorry. I think you should go home."

Colter walked away.

Rebel followed more slowly. Every few steps, her head swung back toward Kensie, still standing outside the police station.

He was a jerk. He knew it. Yeah, some of his words had been true, probably even the part about her being selfish. She just assumed she understood him because she'd seen him limp. Instead of asking what he'd gone through, she'd been focused on her own pain.

Then again, hadn't he done the same thing? Walking away right now was only partly because her mission was likely to end in heartbreak for her and he didn't want to see it. The rest was because she was slowly pulling him back into the world.

He knew part of healing would require him to re-enter the world. And it wasn't because his therapists had told him so, back when the military had tried to force him to get some help. He wasn't blind to the fact that the way he was living wasn't the healthiest choice. But it was a choice that had brought him some measure of peace. Certainly more peace than he'd had in the hospital or even back with his family and friends.

Their platitudes and insistence they knew what he was going through hadn't made him feel loved. It had made him angry. Because no one who hadn't lived through a war and lost people could understand.

Maybe that had been part of the appeal of helping Kensie. She *didn't* know about his past. And he'd thrown that fact in her face.

He squeezed his eyes shut, slowing to a stop. He sensed Rebel pause beside him, always his loyal companion.

Holding in a curse, he glanced back. Just like he knew it would, guilt flooded him at seeing Kensie standing there.

She looked lost and alone. But she also looked unbeaten. Her head was still held high, her shoulders stiff. She wasn't going to give up on Alanna, no matter the odds.

He understood her loyalty. He admired it.

Semper Fi. It was the Marines' battle call, their motto. It was one of his own core beliefs.

Opening his eyes, he turned slowly. Rebel spun with more glee, her tail batting back and forth, slapping against his thigh.

With every step back toward Kensie, his heart pounded harder, warning him this was a mistake.

Already, she was making him feel things that were dangerous. Connection to a mission, connection to another person.

He didn't want to care. He didn't want to re-enter the world, because eventually that would make him face the things he'd lost, face the grief over the *people* he'd lost.

He wanted to stay up in his cabin with Rebel. He wanted to let the peace of the mountains soothe his soul. He'd planned to stay there the rest of his life. He knew it would be lonely, especially after Rebel was gone. But that seemed like the safest choice, the happiest choice for him.

As he approached, Kensie watched him warily, probably with no idea what she was doing to his life.

"I'm sorry." His voice creaked with emotion and embarrassment heated his cheeks.

Rebel shoved her head under Kensie's hand, tail wagging enthusiastically.

A surprised laugh burst from Kensie at Rebel's antics and in that moment, Colter wanted to move forward. He wanted to laugh like that, un-constrained and free. He wanted to spend time with a woman like Kensie. If this had been a year ago, not only would he have done everything in his power to help her, no matter the odds, but he would also have pursued her. Hard.

She still looked wary, as though she wasn't sure

she wanted to accept his apology. As though she wasn't sure she wanted his help. "Colter…"

The idea of venturing back into the world, even this tiny bit with her, scared him. Terrified him might be more accurate. But he'd made the decision now, and he shouldn't have turned away just because she hadn't been totally up-front with him.

He'd accepted a mission. And whether or not it was one that could be accomplished, he owed it to her to try.

He owed it to himself, too. To see if he could really do it.

He cut off whatever response she had to his apology by stepping forward into her personal space. Close, so she wouldn't misunderstand.

She froze, her mouth still open.

He didn't hesitate. He wrapped an arm around her waist and yanked her to him before he could think better of it.

Kensie stumbled, but his bad leg didn't protest much as he caught her weight against his body. Then he captured her lips with his.

She tasted like coffee and peppermint. She tasted like every dream he'd ever had for himself, before his world was torn apart.

His other arm wrapped around her, pulling her even tighter against him, and then he lost himself. For a moment, everything else disappeared. The past, his brothers, her sister, even the inevitable end of knowing her when she returned to Chicago. For a moment, he was living again. Truly living.

Every inch of his body seemed to come alive as her hands slid slowly over his chest and hooked around his neck. She was tall for a woman, but still a good five inches shorter than he was, so when she went up on tiptoes to give him better access, his knees almost buckled. And not because of his injury.

He might have thought it was the fact that he hadn't kissed a woman in over a year. But it wasn't. It was Kensie. The smell of her, some faintly spicy perfume filling his nostrils. The feel of her, little more than an outline through her thick coat. The soft sounds she was making in the back of her throat as she started to kiss him back.

It was less than twenty degrees out here, but he was fast becoming as overheated as he'd been those first days serving in the desert. The thought sent his heart into overdrive, memories of his friends in happier times mingling with Kensie, with the way she was clinging to him.

It was all too much.

Colter let himself have one more taste of her and then he pulled back, breathing hard. Staring down into her dazed eyes, he tried to get hold of himself.

"I'm sorry," he breathed, barely able to speak.

Confusion knitted her forehead and then she tipped her chin up. "I'm not."

She tapped the side of her leg like she'd probably seen him do to get Rebel to follow, then headed toward his truck. When he didn't immediately move, she glanced back, her hair flipping over her shoulder, full of sass. "You coming?"

Rebel was staring up at him, too, her expression plaintive, her tail sweeping slowly, clearing snow from the road.

After that kiss, she thought he might not follow? Still feeling as though his heart might pound its way right out of his chest, Colter hurried after her.

He barely even felt his leg.

Chapter Six

Kensie had hardly slept last night as thoughts of the kiss she'd shared with Colter played over and over in her mind. Instead, she'd tossed and turned in her surprisingly plush, comfortable hotel bed a few miles outside of Desparre. The outside looked like an enormous log cabin, but the inside was as opulent as anywhere she'd been in Chicago.

According to the manager, the hotel attracted mostly tourists from out of state during the summer months. They'd hoped to make Desparre a destination spot, a look at the "true" Alaska. Instead, they were slowly failing, the manager had whispered to her sadly. Kensie had the hotel practically to herself.

She should have felt pampered. But all she'd wanted to do was drive out to another log cabin, this one much smaller and filled with the overwhelming presence of a man who was no good for her.

She still couldn't believe he'd kissed her. Yes, she'd felt his reciprocated attraction from the start.

But he was broken, possibly even more broken than she was.

He hadn't shared much about his time in the military besides his role and the fact that he'd been a soldier for almost a decade. Maybe he just didn't know how to do anything else. Or maybe the soldier in him couldn't live with a physical disability.

Kensie didn't care about his physical limitations. But she did know two things: he was too emotionally damaged to be relationship material, even if she was looking, and she couldn't let him distract her from this chance to find Alanna.

Right now, still yawning from her sleepless night, Kensie darted a furtive glance at Colter. He walked beside her, Rebel between them, near the store where Alanna's note had been found. The plan this morning was to canvass the nearby stores, see if they could find someone who knew anything.

Colter looked like he hadn't slept any better than she had. With his light skin, the circles under his eyes seemed even more prominent. Every twenty feet or so, his right leg dragged a little. For him to even let her see that much, she figured it was hurting him badly. That could have been the reason for both his lack of sleep and his grumpiness.

But she suspected the latter had more to do with the kiss they'd shared last night. When he'd picked her up downtown this morning, he'd handed her a disposable cup with the scent of coffee wafting from it and given her a gruff nod hello. Not exactly the slow, intimate smile she'd been expecting, but maybe it was a good thing.

Except right now, his continued brooding was beginning to annoy her. She didn't want to be ungrateful for his help, but she also didn't want to tiptoe around him.

"Maybe we should split up."

He frowned at her with the most direct eye contact he'd given her all morning. "Why?"

She pointed up ahead at the two businesses sharing a parking lot: a snowplow store and a diner that smelled like grease even from a distance. "We'll accomplish more, faster."

He grunted like he didn't believe her explanation, but she was actually grateful as he and Rebel headed off to the diner. The man may have been emotionally unavailable, but he was also six foot two of muscled temptation. Her willpower was pretty good, but even in his bad mood, walking beside him had made her unusually aware of his every move.

Time to focus on Alanna, Kensie reminded herself as she pushed open the door to the snowplow supply store. As the heavy door slammed closed behind her, she stared in awe. It was more like a warehouse than a store, filled with machines that dwarfed her. At the far end she saw a huge garage door and a checkout counter.

While most of the people she'd met in Desparre looked like they'd either been here forever or the extreme weather had aged them before their time, the guy manning the counter was young. Maybe twenty, with three piercings on his face and tattoos snaking out of both sleeves. He looked like part-time help.

She forced a friendly smile onto her face as she approached. Years of pleas on news stations and talk shows beside her parents, of trailing behind them as they questioned potential witnesses, had taught her that people responded to two things: a friendly approach and a sob story.

This was the part she hated most, selling out her memories of Alanna in the hopes of bringing her sister home. But if it worked, it was worth every sleazy guy who'd offered to "cheer her up," every ambitious reporter who'd salivated at the idea of broadcasting her grief to as many people as possible. It was worth every missed opportunity, every failed relationship. Even every possible relationship, cut off before it could begin.

"Hi," she started. "I'm Kensie Morgan. I'm looking for my sister and—"

The kid shook his head, already going back to the handheld game partially hidden under the counter. "No woman's been through here today."

"It wouldn't have been today. A few weeks ago, a note was left at Jasper's General Store down the road and—"

"You're looking for the kidnapped girl?" His head snapped back up, the game forgotten. "The news said she's been missing for fourteen years."

"That's right. She has dark hair like mine. And brown eyes, a little darker than mine." Were those things still true? Kensie assumed so, but had no way to really know. Maybe Alanna's hair had been dyed or she wore colored contacts. Or maybe, now that they were all grown up, they looked nothing alike anymore.

The kid shrugged. "I only started here this week. I guess the last guy just walked out and didn't come back, so here I am. It's great, pretty quiet so I can do my homework."

Kensie's hopes sank. "So you don't know if the owner saw anyone like that over the past few weeks, maybe around the time the note was left?"

"Sorry. But can I ask you—"

"Thanks." She cut him off, not wanting to hear his questions about what had happened to her sister or what she worried had happened in all the years Alanna had been gone. Even the people who were sympathetic usually didn't know how to walk the line between support and morbid curiosity. That line was a lot thinner than most people realized.

As she headed back the way she'd come, the door opened and a man as tall as Colter, but who looked a decade and a half older, walked in. "Hey, where's Derrick?" he yelled across the store.

"Not working today," the kid called back.

"Excuse me," Alanna said, her hopes lifting again. "Do you live around here?"

"Yeah." The man turned deep brown eyes on her as he drew out the word, scowling.

That angry scowl. It was vaguely familiar. Kensie's heart rate picked up as she realized why. It reminded her of the man who'd taken Alanna.

Fourteen years ago, he'd climbed out of the passenger seat of a dark blue sedan, wearing all blue—jeans and a lightweight sweater. His long arms had stretched out and yanked her sister right off her feet. Alanna had let out a muffled squeak and then Kensie had screamed loudly enough that it should have brought the entire city running.

He'd met her gaze for mere seconds. She hadn't been able to tell his eye color from across the yard, but he'd been scowling. A deep, intense scowl she'd never forget. He'd been about the age this guy would have been back then, too. His hair had been more brown, whereas this guy had streaks of gray, but that might have just been time.

Kensie let out a small laugh, earning her a perplexed—and slightly concerned—look from the man. It was weird, but she'd done this repeatedly over the years. She'd see someone on the street and everything in her would go unnaturally still, even her breathing. Then adrenaline would kick in, sending her heart and mind into overdrive. A few minutes later, she'd come to her senses. The psychiatrist her parents had forced her to see for a few sessions as a kid had given it a name, but Kensie couldn't remember it.

She'd gotten such a brief look at Alanna's kidnapper. She probably wouldn't have been able to identify him fourteen years ago, let alone now.

The man started to walk away and Kensie grabbed his arm, surprised at the ropey strength beneath the thick jean jacket. His arm flexed and he jerked it free, almost knocking her down.

"You need something, lady?" He looked her up and down, studying her too intently. He might have been good-looking in some circumstances, but the anger curling his lips and raking harsh lines across his forehead ruined it.

She held her hands up. "Sorry. It's just—you've lived here awhile?"

"Yeah, why?"

She tried a smile, hoping it would soften him up. "You know the regulars, it sounds like, and I'm looking for someone."

He shifted, angling away from her. His gaze darted from the kid behind the counter to the big garage door at the other end of the space. Then he stared back at her suspiciously. "Who?"

"My sister. She was kidnapped a long time ago."

"Your sister, huh?" He scowled some more. "From where?"

"The Midwest." The words came out without

conscious thought. Normally she said Chicago, but even telling herself she was being crazy, something about this guy was getting her radar up. He might just be unfriendly. Or maybe he actually knew something and she needed to tread carefully. Would getting too specific about Alanna—if he actually did know her, if by some crazy fluke he really was the person who'd grabbed her all those years ago—scare him away?

The guy's head swiveled back and forth between the doors again. "I don't know your sister, lady."

"But—"

He spun back the way he'd come, darting a glance over his shoulder as he threw the door open, then practically ran outside.

Kensie swore under her breath then ran after him, yanking her phone out of her pocket. She skidded to a stop in the snow outside as he leaped into a truck.

With shaky hands, she snapped a photo of him. For one second, he froze, like he might jump out and rip the phone from her hands. Then the truck flew backward out of the lot, and slammed to a stop before changing direction and racing away.

He needed to get out more.

The thought surprised Colter. Usually, when he came to town and people wanted to ask him questions about his life or make small talk, he couldn't wait to get back to his cabin and shut the rest of the world out.

But today, carrying a homemade chocolate chip cookie that the grandfather of seven who owned the diner had given him, while Rebel drooled happily over a dog biscuit, Colter felt lighter than he had in a long time. His steps picked up as he headed toward the store where he'd left Kensie.

Once upon a time, she would have been everything he wanted. Back then, he'd been the kind of guy who'd had a map of his life drawn in his mind. He might have taken one look at her and sensed the possibility for marriage and kids. For a home waiting for him in between military tours.

That was the life he'd always imagined for himself. The kind of life his brothers in the Marines had: video calls with spouses, letters written in crayon arriving at bases around the world, pictures to carry inside their helmets. Something to fight for. Someone to go home to.

He'd never have any of that now. Without the military, the vision was a mess. He couldn't imagine a sedate life for himself, with a woman who didn't mind picking up the slack when his injury got to be too much, and kids who didn't mind that their dad couldn't run after them like other dads. If he was being honest, he didn't want that life at all now.

He'd come to Alaska not just to hide, but also to heal. Somehow, over the past year, he'd lost sight of the *healing* part. But Kensie had forced him out of his comfort zone, out of the solitude of his cabin, and it was reminding him of why he loved it here. Why he'd chosen it in the first place.

Sure, there were guys like Danny Weston, people who'd come here to take advantage of Alaska's wide-open spaces and hide from whatever terrible thing they'd done. But there were also people like the grandfather who'd owned this diner for the past thirty years. Hardworking people who'd come here for the chance to live a simpler life, to connect with nature and themselves. That's what he wanted.

Kissing Kensie last night had reignited in him all the old dreams and this morning he'd woken with what felt like a hangover. The inevitable disappointment he felt whenever he dreamed of the past. Waking up and remembering it was all gone had spiraled him into depression more than once. He wasn't going there again.

Kensie was never going to be anything more to him than a memory. But maybe her entering his life was exactly the kick in the butt he needed to make him rejoin the world.

No, life was never going to be the way he'd imagined when he was eighteen and just embarking on his first military tour. But how many people's lives turned out the way they planned when they were little more than kids?

At his side, Rebel trotted along happily, with

nothing left of her biscuit but a lone crumb on the top of her nose. A smile trembled on his lips. He could still be happy here. Just because his trajectory had changed didn't mean it was pointless. He could find meaning in his life, allow himself to enjoy the solitude of his cabin, the endless open views across the valley.

He drew in a deep, cold breath of Alaskan air. It was time to face his future.

Chapter Seven

Kensie had barely spoken to him since he'd picked her up at the snowplow store.

Colter shot another glance at her across the truck cab. He hadn't known her long, but she wasn't usually this quiet. And while it could have been his own bad mood from when he'd met up with her a few hours ago causing her silence, he didn't think so.

It was probably the kiss they'd shared.

For the hundredth time since it had happened, he cursed himself. But this time it was half-hearted. How could he fully regret something that had reset his perspective on his life? Yeah, maybe kissing her had been a lapse in judgment, but hopefully it was the push he needed to get his life in order. To figure out how he was going to truly make this place his home, instead of just his hideout.

He gripped the wheel a little tighter, trying to find the right words. He'd never had to apologize for kissing someone before.

Eyes still on the icy road in front of him, Colter started, "The past year, I've been hiding out in my cabin. Not really on purpose. But I came here for the solitude and it was easy to turn that into a solitary life."

He glanced at her to see if she'd figured out where he was going with this meandering opening salvo, but she was just staring out the windshield, forehead furrowed. So he kept going. "Helping you wasn't easy for me. I know you don't get it, but trust me when I say that any kind of mission was the last thing I thought I needed."

She was silent, so he pushed forward, faster now, starting to feel foolish for not just blurting a simple apology and leaving it at that. "That's why I bailed on you when I found out you weren't telling me everything. And when I kissed you..."

Kensie stayed silent, lips pursed like she was waiting for a real apology. Or maybe she wasn't even listening to him. It was hard to tell.

"I'm sorry. I should have—"

"It was a mistake. I get it. I agree. We got carried away in the moment. It's not like it's going to happen again." Kensie cut him off suddenly, swiveling in her seat as far as the seatbelt would let her. She tucked one knee up underneath her, facing him even as Rebel tried to stick her nose in between to be petted.

It wasn't going to happen again? Even though that had been his plan, too, hearing her say the words made him long to pull the truck over and see if she really meant it.

Visions of her kissing him filled his head. The way she'd fit inside the circle of his arms, soft and feminine but stronger than he'd expected. The way her lips had melded instantly to his, like she'd been imagining it since the moment he'd first helped her up off the icy Desparre street.

Then the vision shifted, moved into territory he had no business imagining. Of her back at his cabin, standing in front of the fire as she dropped her coat to the floor. As his fingers found their way underneath the hem of her sweater and his lips traced a path from her mouth down to the pulse at her neck. As he lingered there, pulling her body closer until there was barely any space between them.

"I think I might have just met Alanna's kidnapper."

It took a minute for him to process Kensie's words, for them to penetrate the increasingly erotic vision in his head. Once they did, he slowed the truck to a stop, pulling over as far as he could, and turned to face her. "What?"

"I know it sounds crazy and at first I thought I was just imagining things." Kensie spoke at warp speed, reaching out to clutch his arm as if to keep his interest.

As if that was a problem. "Who is it? Why

didn't you come and get me?" And why was she just now mentioning this?

"I don't know his name, but I got his picture." She let go of his arm to fumble in her pocket and pull out her phone.

When she turned it to show him, he squinted at it a long minute, trying to place the guy. "I recognize him. He's lived here a long time." Colter tried to come up with a name, but couldn't. "I think he's got a place on the outskirts of Desparre somewhere. Comes in periodically for supplies. Usually to the spot we just visited, not the main part of town." He lifted his gaze from the phone. "Did you ask the store owner, Derrick? He could probably tell you this guy's name."

Kensie shook her head. "Derrick wasn't there. Just a kid who was working the counter."

"So, this guy who came into the store for supplies…why do you think he has Alanna?"

"He looked familiar."

Colter tried to keep the disbelief off his face. She'd been just a child when her sister had been kidnapped. "You got a good look at the guy back then? How close were you?"

How close had she come to being grabbed alongside Alanna? The idea made him nauseous.

"I was across the yard. I wasn't close enough to help her."

Kensie's voice was so mournful that Colter reached out without thinking and twined his fingers with hers. She clutched tight instantly, as if by instinct, and his heart pounded harder.

"You were thirteen years old, Kensie. What could you have done?" Besides get herself kidnapped—or worse?

"I should have done something. It was my responsibility to watch out for her that day!"

"That's not fair, Kensie. You can't carry that burden." He stared into her eyes, watching them darken with anger or frustration. Who was he to talk about the burden of survivor's guilt? But when it came to this, he knew he was right, so he pressed forward. "And look what kind of sister you've been. All these years later and you're here, searching for her, when even law enforcement won't."

It didn't seem possible, but she squeezed his hand even tighter. "Thank you for helping me," she whispered.

Kissing her yesterday had been a mistake. He knew it. But that didn't stop him from wanting to lean forward and do it again right now.

It took more willpower than he'd thought he had to resist that urge. Instead, he asked, "How sure are you about this guy you saw in the store?"

She let out a humorless laugh. "Not sure at all. But he *ran* when I asked him about my sister."

Colter frowned. He didn't even know the guy's name and yet he couldn't imagine the loner being a child kidnapper. But even though Desparre locals tended to be wary of strangers, running away from questions was suspicious. And, absolutely, something sounded off about the guy.

The question was, had Kensie spooked him? If so, would he run before they could figure out if he had Alanna?

"EITHER HE'S THE one who kidnapped Alanna or he knows who did." Kensie spoke the words with certainty, tapping the picture she'd snapped before the guy had run away from her as fast as he could.

Colter frowned, like he was unconvinced.

But still, he'd brought her here, to a cozy restaurant-slash-food-store halfway between the snow supply warehouse and downtown. Apparently, the owner had lived in the area all his life and Colter claimed if anyone could tell them more about their suspect, it was him.

Their suspect. It sounded like something a detective would say, one of the overworked, tired-looking officers assigned to Alanna's case. *We have a suspect, but don't get your hopes up.* She'd heard those words a few times over the years, but they'd never led anywhere, even though she'd *always* gotten her hopes up.

This time had to be different. She refused to consider any other possibility. She wasn't sure she could handle another disappointment.

Just the idea of returning home without Alanna made pain lodge behind her breastbone, where it always did when she thought about how long her sister had been gone. Over the years, she'd had moments where she'd felt like maybe she could come to terms with the cold, hard statistics that said Alanna was long dead. But those moments were always fleeting, either because the idea was too much to bear or because she and her sister had always shared a special connection. Wouldn't she feel it in her heart if Alanna was gone?

The idea was foolish. Intellectually, she knew it. But she still believed.

"What are you thinking?"

Colter's words broke into her thoughts and Kensie looked up at him. Backlit by one of the restaurant's cozy lamps, which brought out the gold in his hair and softened the sharp lines of his face, he looked even sexier than usual. Her stomach flipped around for a different reason. Why couldn't she meet a man like this back in Chicago, with Colter's intensity and dedication, but without all of the baggage weighing on him so heavily she could practically see it?

"I'm thinking this has to be the break I need." Her words came out soft, almost sultry, and Kensie cleared her throat, ashamed of herself for lusting after Colter when all of her attention needed to be on Alanna.

To distract herself, she reached down and Rebel obligingly sat up, giving her easy access to stroke the dog's soft fur. Apparently, either Alaska was lenient about pet rules or everyone just knew and liked Rebel. She suspected the latter. Despite what people had told her about Colter not getting out much, the town seemed to be small enough that everyone knew of him and Rebel, if not the details of their lives.

"I hope so," Colter replied, but the lines between his eyebrows told her that her optimism worried him.

He probably figured she'd break if it turned out to be a dead end. If only he knew how many dead ends she'd survived over the years. Then again, she wasn't sure she had it in her to survive another.

Instead of replying, Kensie glanced around the lodge. She didn't have to look far.

The man approaching—with his long gray beard, weathered skin and seen-it-all gaze—had to be the owner. He shook Colter's hand, gave Rebel a slight frown, then glanced at Kensie. "New to Alaska?"

"Yes, I'm—"

"We're wondering if you could help us with something." Colter cut her off. He grabbed her phone and held it up. "You know this guy?"

The owner glanced from the phone to her and back again. "Seen him around over the years. Can't say I know his name. He's not really a talkative sort. Keeps to himself, seems to like it that way. You must understand the feeling."

Colter just lifted an eyebrow, but Kensie sighed, disappointed. "We should track down the owner of the snowplow shop. This guy was yelling his name when he came in. They know each other. Maybe the store owner knows where to find him."

"Why are you looking for him?" the owner prodded.

"I think—"

"We just need his help with something." Colter stood, dropping some money on the table for the cocoas they'd ordered but barely touched. Beside her, Rebel stood, watching Colter attentively. "Any chance you can tell us how to find Derrick Notte?"

"Guy who owns the snowplow place? Yeah, I can give you his address." He stared hard at Colter, ignoring Kensie and Rebel altogether. "But you piss him off and we're going to have problems."

Colter smiled, but it was hard and uncompromising. "He's not the one I'm planning to piss off."

The owner stared a minute longer, then let out a snort of laughter. "All right. Why don't you finish your drinks and I'll get the address."

Colter nodded and sat back down. Rebel followed suit, settling back on her hind legs.

Kensie lowered herself into her chair more slowly, waiting until the owner had walked away to whisper, "What was that about?"

"People like their privacy out here. He's giving

me Derrick's home address on faith. If Derrick gets mad about it, he'll start something."

"Seems a little dramatic," Kensie muttered.

"Yeah, it is. But I didn't want him to know what you were thinking. People out here don't like it when you assume the worst about us."

"I'm not," Kensie protested. "It's not a generalization. It's just this guy looks like—"

"I know," Colter cut her off. "But he didn't, and I didn't want to get into it. People here will help you if you need it, but they've got a live-and-let-live attitude. You probably hear about the ones running from the law, but we get the other side of it, too."

"What does that mean? People like you?"

Colter's lips twisted. "Yeah, I guess. I meant more like people running from someone who's hurt them. They rely on the residents here to respect their privacy. Domestic violence survivors, victims of stalkers, things like that."

"Oh." Kensie stared out the window of the restaurant at dense, snowy woods. The guy at the rental car place had told her Desparre had a higher population of bears than it did people. A smart place to hide from someone who wanted to do you harm. But too easy for a kidnapper to hide away with his victim, too.

"Kensie, can I ask you something?"

She refocused on the man across from her, and

the serious expression on his face made her nervous. "Okay."

"There's something that's been bothering me since you first told me about your sister's note."

"What is it?" She almost didn't want to know the answer. It felt like the trajectory of her entire life was riding on the outcome of this note.

Colter must have sensed her distress, because he set down his mug of cocoa, reached across the table and took her hand. His roughened fingers rubbed over her palm, sending shivers up her arm.

It was the kind of thing a boyfriend would do. Not a guy you'd just met who'd agreed to be your guide in the Alaskan wilderness. Kensie tried to ignore the emotions he was stirring up.

"If the note is really from your sister, why did she walk into a store and leave a message, but not run or ask for help? Surely if she was in distress or someone had her immobilized, she never would have been able to leave the note at all without the store owner noticing."

Kensie nodded, staring down at their joined hands. It had bothered her from the beginning, too, and for two entirely different reasons.

Taking a deep breath, she met his gaze. "It might be a sign that the note is fake." The possibility hurt, and she didn't want to even consider it, but she knew it was there.

Years of coordinating with law enforcement and private cold-case groups had also taught her the other possibility, which in some ways was even worse. "Or it could mean she's so afraid of her kidnapper or so conditioned to obey him that even given the chance to run, she won't take it."

In Colter's eyes, she saw understanding and sadness. As a soldier, he'd probably seen cases like that, captives who'd been tortured so badly that even when they saw a chance to escape, they were too terrified to try.

If that was what had happened with her sister— if the note was a final, desperate plea for someone to find her because she couldn't manage to run on her own—what shape would she be in if they located her?

Would the Alanna she'd known still be in there? Or would the woman Alanna had become be a hollow shell of the girl she'd once been?

If that was the case, Kensie wasn't sure either of them would ever recover from what happened in Desparre.

Chapter Eight

Kensie was discouraged.

He never should have asked her about the note. If Colter had been thinking, he would have realized the implications without her having to tell him.

He didn't like that she knew what it meant. Not that he thought she was naive or clueless, but as much as he didn't want a connection, he couldn't deny that he cared about Kensie. Hopefully she wouldn't be in Desparre for long. He wanted a happy ending for her and her sister. He wished she'd had an uncomplicated life, without sorrow or tragedy.

Those things were for soldiers like him.

It was a ridiculous, unrealistic way to think, but there it was. He'd become a soldier for a lot of reasons, but one of them was because he wanted to make a difference. He liked to protect people. And that instinct was kicking up harder than usual with Kensie.

Apparently Rebel felt the same way, because

even though she wasn't supposed to, she swiveled on her butt and dropped her head into Kensie's lap. Kensie looked surprised for a second, then laughed and started petting his dog again.

If he wasn't careful, Rebel was going to want to follow Kensie back to Chicago. If he wasn't careful, he was going to want to do the same thing.

Colter pushed out the crazy thought and tried to distract Kensie. After they'd talked to the restaurant owner, she'd wanted to drive immediately out to Derrick's house. But his question had gotten her upset and he didn't want her going to Derrick's that way. The guy was prickly on his best day. He'd be a huge pain if Kensie was confrontational. Especially since Colter knew *he* was likely to become confrontational if Derrick didn't cooperate. If they were going to get answers out of the guy, they needed Kensie's soft touch.

So, he'd ordered the restaurant's famous wild berry cobbler and pushed the plate toward her as soon as it arrived. She'd only picked at it initially, but the longer they'd sat, the bigger her bites had gotten. The place was famous for its cobbler for a reason.

"Tell me about your sister. What was she like?" Colter asked now, hoping to fill her mind with good memories she could draw on to win over Derrick if needed.

Kensie paused, a bite of cobbler halfway to her mouth. A sad smile tugged her lips. "She was goofy and fun. Even at five, we were already predicting she'd be homecoming queen or class president when she got older. Probably both. She was always the center of attention, always in the middle of the party. It was funny, because both me and Flynn—who's halfway between me and Alanna in age—were shy and serious. Bookish, my mom called us."

Colter smiled, because that wasn't how he saw Kensie at all. Maybe she'd outgrown her shyness or maybe she had an inaccurate perception of herself as a child, but she drew people to her with ease. He couldn't picture her ever being on the sidelines.

"Before Alanna went missing, I was teaching her to play violin." Kensie's smile turned wistful. "She'd seen me play and she wanted to be just like me."

"You were close?"

"Yeah. We were eight years apart, but we always had a special bond. Whenever I play now, I think of Alanna."

"You still play?"

"I'm a violinist in an orchestra back home. That's my job." Suddenly seeming to realize she'd been holding a forkful of cobbler, Kensie stuffed it into her mouth.

She played at such a high level that she did it for a living? He pictured her with a violin in her hand, bow flying across the strings, her eyes intense with concentration. "I'd love to hear you play."

Kensie's lips tipped upward, but there was still sadness in her eyes. She swallowed and told him, "I don't have my violin."

Of course not. It was back at home, with the rest of her family. A family who was probably waiting anxiously for Kensie to return—and hopefully bring with her the sister they hadn't seen in fourteen years.

It was a huge responsibility to carry alone.

He wanted to promise her they'd find Alanna. That he'd help her carry that load. But he knew it was an empty promise, so he didn't say it. Sure, he'd do what he could to give her access to the locals, to get her safely wherever she needed to go. But that was as much as he could do, and he knew it was nothing compared to what she needed. Compared to what she deserved.

"Why don't you have a boyfriend or a husband up here with you?"

The question was rude, and he regretted it the instant it came out of his mouth. Even Rebel lifted her head from Kensie's lap to eye him over the table, as if she disapproved.

"Sorry. None of my business," he said before she could answer.

"No boyfriend or husband. It's hard to…"

She trailed off, and it took him a minute to catch up and wonder what was hard about it, because he was too busy being pleased she wasn't attached. Which was selfish, because he had no claim on her and never would.

"What about you?"

"Why aren't I married?" The words popped out of his mouth full of surprise—both that she'd ask and that she didn't already know. He was broken.

"No," she said quickly, a flush rushing up her cheeks. "What do you do for a living?"

Half-relieved he didn't have to wade into that minefield and half-disappointed that she wasn't interested, Colter shrugged. "Since I left the military, I've been writing pieces for newspapers and magazines."

It was part-time work he sometimes loved and sometimes hated. He loved being able to share his perspective, to give civilians a more accurate look into how the military worked. But it reminded him that he wasn't where he belonged, in the middle of the action. It reminded him that he'd never be there again.

"The job is permanent?" she asked, probably picking up on his hesitation.

It was funny that he'd ended up writing, since his parents had always pushed him toward a career in communications. But it wasn't his passion, just a way to pay the bills. "Nah."

"So, what's next?"

He frowned, his instinct not to answer. But

she'd been honest with him, so it was only fair he do the same. "I don't know."

Most of his life, he'd had a goal. He'd known from an early age he wanted to join the military, fascinated by stories from his grandfather, who'd lived in Poland during World War Two. He'd tried to help people escape, gotten caught and been thrown into the gulag in Siberia for his efforts.

His grandfather hadn't fought in the war. But he'd seen it firsthand and the injustices he'd described had made Colter long to change the world. It was a child's wish, but it had matured into a man's desire to make some kind of difference for people who couldn't do it for themselves.

When he'd enlisted right out of high school, his parents had been shocked. They'd been so sure he'd grow out of what they considered a childish dream. But to him, it was all he'd ever wanted. Being a man without a mission was an uncomfortable feeling.

But even more so was this new mission he found himself on, helping Kensie. Because the more she pulled him back into the world, the more he realized he was going to have to figure it out. He couldn't go back to the military. That part of his life was over, whether he wanted it to be or not.

He'd never again be Staff Sergeant Hayes. Now he was simply Colter. What exactly that meant, he wasn't sure. Once he'd helped her, he needed to move on and figure out what was next for him.

It was easier said than done. Desparre wasn't exactly teeming with opportunities for a guy who had no experience doing anything except being a soldier.

"Well, what about your family?" Kensie asked.

"What about them?"

"What do they think you should do next?"

"I have no idea. Move back home, probably." He hadn't asked and his parents hadn't suggested anything. He'd never thought about it before, but it was strange. They'd tried so hard to convince him not to join up. Once he'd come home damaged, they'd done their best to get him to return to the sleepy Idaho town where he was born. When he'd come here, instead, it was as if they'd finally given up trying.

Kensie was frowning, so he tried to explain. "I'm an only child. They had me late in life and in some ways I think they never quite knew what to do with me."

She frowned even harder, so he rushed on, "Don't get me wrong. They love me. They just never understood me. Never got why I wanted to join the military or what I was looking for there. The military gave me a mission, camaraderie and a brotherhood. I know it's different than your bond with your sister, because I didn't grow up with them, but it's a brotherhood all the same."

He trailed off, wondering how he'd gotten onto this subject. The faces of his lost brothers flashed in his mind and he gulped in a deep breath, praying he wasn't about to go into panic mode.

Rebel whimpered, scooting out from where she'd cozied up to Kensie to come around and nudge him. She was good at that, nudging him back to the present. Nudging him out of his panic.

Colter grounded himself by fisting his hand in her soft fur. He blew out the breath, focusing on evening out his heartbeat. It slowed and Kensie came back into focus, looking worried.

"I'm fine," he said before she could ask. "Hard subject."

"Why?" she asked slowly, like she was afraid she already knew the answer.

Colter pushed the words out fast, not wanting to linger on them. "They're all gone. Every one of my brothers, dead in an ambush. I'm the only one still here and it's not right. I should have gone with them that day."

COLTER THOUGHT HE should be dead?

Kensie had been shocked into silence at his admission, especially after Colter dropped that secret and then hadn't said another word about it. Even now, half an hour after he'd first told her, she was at a loss for words. She hadn't even known him for two days, but already she couldn't imagine the world without him.

And yet, how could she say that without sounding like she was infatuated with him or coddling him? Not to mention that now she felt horrible about the assumptions she'd made, thinking he was just hiding out in Alaska because he'd been injured.

She'd said terrible things to him when he'd gotten mad because she wasn't up-front about the FBI's assessment. Things about him not understanding loss, about how he should just *get over* his trauma. As if you could ever just get over losing your family, whether it was blood-related or chosen.

At least with Alanna there was still a chance. Still hope. Colter didn't even have that much.

"I'm so sorry," she said, and her voice came out a pitiful whisper as he pulled his truck up to Derrick's big log house. Her attempt at sympathy felt so insignificant next to what Colter had endured, and she knew she'd waited too long to say anything at all, trying to find the right words. As if there were any right words for that kind of loss.

He gave her a quick, sideways glance. "Not your fault," he answered briskly, flinging open his door. He stepped out and slammed it shut before she could say anything else.

Kensie glanced at Rebel, ashamed of herself, and the dog stared solemnly back at her until Colter opened the rear door and slapped his leg. Then she hopped out, leaving Kensie alone.

Focus, Kensie reminded herself. She had time to figure out how to give Colter a proper apology, since he was still helping her. Right now, she needed her attention to be on convincing Derrick to give them information.

Because the guy she'd seen at his store was connected to Alanna somehow. Kensie could feel it in her gut, as strong as the instinct screaming that Alanna was still here, that the note was real. That Alanna was still alive. Just waiting for Kensie to bring her home.

Kensie squeezed her eyes shut, praying she was right. Then she opened them and stepped out of the truck, hurrying up the unshoveled drive after Colter.

Derrick's house was nothing like Colter's, besides being a log cabin. It was at least twice as big, and the much smaller windows in front were all covered by shades. Still, Derrick must have heard them coming because the door opened before Colter could knock.

If ever she'd imagined a mountain man of Alaska, this is what she would have pictured. Derrick was huge—more wide than tall—with snow-white hair and an unkempt matching beard. He wore pants with a bulky vinyl appearance that looked like they were made for the outdoors and a thick flannel shirt that barely buttoned over his barrel chest. There was even an unlit cigar clamped in the corner of his mouth.

"What do you want?" he asked out of the side of his mouth not occupied by the cigar.

"We're looking for someone. We're hoping you can help us." Colter held out his hand to Kensie and she silently passed over her phone.

"Do you know this guy?" Colter held up the screen.

"He came to your store today looking for you," Kensie added.

Derrick blinked and then his gaze shifted to her. "Why do you want to know about Henry?"

"His name is Henry?" Kensie shuffled up closer, squishing Rebel between herself and Colter. The dog didn't seem to mind, just looked up at her and then back to Derrick, as if she was waiting for the answer, too. "Henry what?"

"How about you answer my question first, sweetheart," Derrick replied, the emphasis on *sweetheart* making it sound negative instead of an endearment.

Kensie heated with annoyance, but she gritted her teeth and gave him a smile instead. "I think—"

"She thinks Henry might be able to help her find her sister," Colter cut in.

"She can't talk for herself?"

"Let's not start something, Derrick," Colter answered, his voice low and hard.

Derrick smiled around his cigar. "You trying to scare me, soldier?"

"You don't want me trying," Colter shot back just as quickly.

Kensie stepped forward, slightly in front of Rebel, almost in Derrick's face. "Look, I get that you want to protect this guy's privacy, but—"

"Nah, I don't care about that," Derrick cut in. "Henry comes by the shop plenty, 'cause he knows I'll help him out. Advice. Best places to hunt, how to stay below the radar. I don't mind. But it's pretty clear the guy's hiding from something." He darted a sideways glance at Colter. "Then again, isn't everyone?"

"I'm not hiding from the law," Colter said, tipping his head meaningfully.

Derrick's eyes narrowed at Kensie. "He hurt your sister?"

"I don't know." Her voice broke and Kensie cleared her throat, embarrassed. She knew how to do this. She'd done this since she was thirteen years old. It was almost a role: dutiful older sister, willing to show whatever pain or desperation was needed in order to get information.

"Henry Rollings."

"You know where he lives?" Colter asked as Kensie breathed, "Thank you."

Derrick nodded at her, then looked back at Colter. "Up past the snowplow shop. He always comes in from the west. Off that old unmarked trail. Could be anywhere up that way."

Colter looked pensive, then held out his hand. "Thank you."

Derrick shook his hand and told him, "Look after this one."

Kensie stiffened a little at being talked about like she wasn't standing right there, but softened as Colter answered seriously, "It's my top priority."

"Good luck," Derrick told her, then closed the door on them.

Colter turned and headed back to the truck, Rebel trotting after him.

Kensie moved more slowly, staring at his back. This man working so hard to help her thought he shouldn't even be here. The idea filled her with a dangerous desire: to give him something to live for.

Chapter Nine

Kensie was in his bedroom right now. Probably undressed.

The idea made Colter breathe faster and he couldn't keep his gaze from drifting over—yet again—to the closed door between them. No one besides Kensie had ever been inside his cabin. Now she'd been here twice. This time, it had been his idea.

Even though the reasons weren't personal, having her in his space *felt* personal. He imagined her right now, looking around his room. Taking in the simple spindle bed in the middle, Rebel's cushy dog bed in the corner. Maybe the pictures on his nightstand.

One of his parents from his graduation, younger and still convinced he'd change his mind about the military. Grinning with their arms around each other's waists, still madly in love after twenty-five years together. Back then, proud and excited about the future they imagined for him, so different than the path he'd seen for himself.

Another picture of Colter's brothers, taken not long before that final mission. Laughing and smiling, relaxed at the base. None of them knowing they had only a few hours left to live.

The memory sobered him, and images of Kensie changing out of her clothes into something more appropriate for the weather fled. But thoughts of Kensie herself stuck. Having her here didn't feel strange. It felt natural. And that made him nervous.

He had no room for anyone else in his life, especially not a woman whose time in Alaska had an expiration date. Because even though he missed his parents—and there were days he desperately wished he'd followed their dreams for him instead of his own, so he wouldn't know this pain now—he couldn't imagine ever returning to Idaho. Or going anywhere else, for that matter.

In the past year, Alaska had become his home. This cabin calmed him. The wide open spaces and cold, unforgiving weather relaxed him, helped reduce his panic. One day, maybe this place would even heal him, get him partway back to whole again.

The door to his bedroom opened and Kensie lumbered out.

Colter couldn't help the laugh that escaped. After talking to Derrick, she'd wanted to immediately try and track Henry Rollings. But he'd insisted on bringing her back to the main part of Desparre to get clothes more appropriate for Alaska's coming weather.

Instead of dropping her at her hotel, he'd brought her here to change, because he'd wanted to stop off for a different kind of gear himself.

In early October, Desparre might hit twenty-five degrees midday if you were lucky. Lows regularly got down to two degrees. It wasn't really that bad, once you got used to it. But the problem was that Desparre wasn't a city like Chicago, filled with easy places to stop in and warm up if your car broke down or the wind chill got to be too much. October was also the snowiest month of the year and there was no guarantee when the snow would start—or stop. In a few weeks they could be so snowed in that no one was getting out until spring.

Keeping Kensie here until the flowers poked up in the valley below wasn't a half-bad idea. Even how she was dressed now, in boots appropriate for the mountains, snow pants and a jacket that would actually keep her warm if they got stuck out in the cold somewhere, he couldn't take his eyes off her.

She took big, exaggerated steps out of his room, as though she was weighed down by all the gear he'd made her get. But he shook his head, not buying it. Everything he'd picked for her was relatively lightweight.

"I feel like a snow monster," Kensie complained.

"You look cute." He hadn't meant to say it out loud, and her eyes widened. Hoping she wouldn't take that the wrong way, he added, "This is going to be much better if we get stranded somewhere."

"Why would we get stranded?"

"Well, hopefully we won't," Colter said, even though the idea of being stranded anywhere with Kensie didn't sound bad at all. "But weather here can be unpredictable. We get surprised by a blizzard or trapped on the hill by an avalanche and you're going to want real winter gear."

She looked nervous for a second, but then her expression shifted and her thoughts were broadcasted on her face. She'd definitely looked at the pictures in his room, and they'd made her think of his words earlier, about avoiding his rightful fate alongside his brothers. The look on her face now was one of uncertainty, as if she wanted to bring it up again but wasn't sure how. And mixed with that was pity. If there was anything he hated, it was pity.

"Stop staring at me like I'm damaged."

She looked startled. "I'm not."

Rebel lifted her head from the spot she'd claimed near the hearth, her head swiveling between them, cars perked.

He took a few steps toward Kensie. "Yeah, you are." He didn't know why he cared. They both knew it was true, so why did it matter if he could see it on her face? Was it better that she thought it, but kept it hidden?

Still, the idea of her thinking that he was *less* made tension build up inside him. Suddenly he couldn't think of anything he wanted more than to prove he was whole. Or, at least, whole enough.

He was still walking toward her. He hadn't intended to, but the closer he got, the better an idea it seemed. The closer he got, the more her eyes widened and her lips parted.

As he stared at the fullness of her lips, the rapidly increasing rise and fall of her chest, the past seemed to fall away. He reached out, letting his fingers drift over the puffiness of her coat, down to her bare hands. Somehow, with Kensie so covered up, the act of sliding his fingers between hers was intensified. The softness of her skin, the delicate strength in her fingers, calloused from playing violin. Pleasure shot up from the point where their skin met, and he tugged her toward him.

Instead of pulling back like she probably should have, she fell into him. He smiled at how huge her coat suddenly seemed, putting unnatural distance between them. But instead of unzipping it, he just wrapped his arms around her, pulling her in tighter.

Her hands made a slow, jerky ascent up his chest, and with her head tucked close to his shoulder, he wasn't sure if it was desire or uncertainty putting the hitch in her movements. But then she lifted up on tiptoe so they were lined up perfectly, her beautiful eyes staring back at him.

Her lips were only inches away, her breath puffing against his mouth, but he froze, captivated by the pure toffee brown of her eyes, by the mix of emotions in her gaze. Raw desire, yes. But also something softer, more intimate.

If only that metal hadn't torn through his leg. If only those bullets hadn't torn through his friends. He barely knew her, and yet he could imagine if his life had gone a different way. Kensie waiting for him through deployments, her letters putting a smile on his face when he was away in some far-off country like he'd seen with his brothers when they'd gotten messages from home.

As if she could read his mind, Kensie's expression shifted, lines appearing between her eyebrows. Colter didn't want her to think. He didn't want to think, either. He only wanted to feel.

He leaned in, pressed his lips softly to hers, letting her decide. For a second, he thought she'd change her mind. Then her arms looped tight around his neck, her eyes closed and her mouth moved against his.

All the built-up pressure in his chest released and he sighed against her, loving the silky softness of her lips, the raspiness of her tongue seeking his.

It wasn't enough. He pulled her in even tighter, suddenly hating the sensible coat he'd had her buy. He kissed her harder, faster, desperate for more.

She met each stroke of his tongue, her fingers sliding through his short hair, not enough to grasp. She rose even higher on her toes, giving their kiss a new angle.

A different kind of pressure rose inside him. He could lose himself in this woman. Release all his pain and his past and try to forget himself with a few hours of pleasure.

He forced his hands away from her back, shifted them to her hips. Misunderstanding his intent, she tilted her hips toward him, almost changing his mind. But he couldn't do it. Couldn't use her to soothe the aches in his soul any more than he wanted her to do the same with him.

Because whether she thought so or not, this kiss wasn't really about him. It couldn't be. They barely knew each other. But, on some level, they understood each other.

He knew her pain, the way losing her sister must have followed her through her life, a silent, torturous ghost. He knew the razor-thin line between hope and desperation, between love and torment.

Using his grip on her hips to anchor her, he leaned back, simultaneously peeling her off him. "We shouldn't do this."

His voice didn't even sound like his. It was deeper, gruffer than usual.

She blinked back at him, her cheeks flushed bright red and no comprehension in her gaze.

The fog of desire surrounding her made him want to pull her right back in. Instead, he told her, "Maybe I should be dead, but I'm not. So stop looking at me like I am."

Kensie's lips twisted up, lines raking her forehead. "What?"

Her voice wasn't right either. It was breathy, higher pitched. Way too sexy.

He steeled himself, trying not to lean back in. "You heard me."

Then he turned away so she wouldn't see how little this had to do with his proving something. He might have started walking toward her because of that, but it had quickly become something very different.

But not enough. And she deserved better.

Reaching on top of a cabinet, Colter pulled down his shotgun and dug out a box of shells from the drawer. When he felt like he had some control over his emotions, he turned back toward her.

She looked equal parts stunned and confused.

"Let's do this," he said, tapping his leg for Rebel to follow and heading for the door before he could change his mind.

How could a man who didn't think he belonged among the living make her feel so *alive?*

At twenty-seven, she'd had a handful of long-term relationships, even one that her parents had pushed her to make permanent. She'd had a handful of flings, too. But none of them had made her feel even close to what she'd felt with Colter for a few minutes up in his cabin. Minutes he regretted, if his abrupt stop was anything to go by.

He'd strode out of the cabin—with a shotgun, of all things—and Kensie had been left rooted to the floor. It had taken her an embarrassingly long time to get it together and follow.

Now here they were. Back on the edge of town where Derrick's store was located, except this time they were tackling a bigger stretch of stores. It was about the size of downtown Desparre, but the stores were more spread out, tucked away in a maze of side streets. That was Colter's excuse for them to split up and find out if anyone here could give them more precise information about Henry. That, and the fact that it was rapidly getting dark and he wanted her safely back at her hotel before the sun fully set. The reality, she suspected, had to do with that kiss.

It had started out slow, almost like a first kiss, even though they'd already shared one on the street. But then it had shifted. She wasn't sure which one of them had punched the gas, but suddenly, she hadn't been able to get enough of him. It had felt like a million degrees inside her winter gear as he'd heated her up, but she'd been certain she was about to shed all of it. About to fall into bed with a man she hardly knew.

The idea made her cheeks flush even now, and

she'd barely been able to look at him during the drive over. Embarrassment, yes, but also regret. Falling for Colter was a bad idea for so many reasons, and yet she'd take the heartache later for a night with him now.

That's how you feel right this minute, a little voice in her head whispered. *But what about when you're back in Chicago, all by yourself and missing him?*

The idea made her restless, antsy for a glimpse of Colter and Rebel, to reassure herself he was still close. Once he'd parked the truck, he glanced at her, his expression inscrutable, just staring for a long moment. Then he'd suggested she work her magic with some of the townspeople while he went into the rowdy bar and asked around.

As busy as the bar was, the rest of the town felt dead. It was beautiful, like a postcard, with snow blanketing the roofs and lantern-style streetlights lining the dirt roads, but also a little spooky. She turned down a side street, hoping to find someone to talk to. So far, she'd only run into a couple of shop owners and a father and daughter out for a stroll, none of whom knew Henry.

Back in Chicago, she'd be tripping over people. And yet, in some ways, she felt more connected to Colter here than she ever had to anyone in the city. Her apartment was great, a stone's throw from the lake, a brisk walk to work. Back home, she was always on the move. Going full speed from performances to working with cold-case groups to get attention for Alanna's kidnapping to a decently full social life. It was busy, but something was missing. And not just her sister.

She couldn't remember the last time she'd slowed down and really enjoyed life. Since she'd been in Desparre, she'd been moving at warp speed, too, searching for any possible leads before it was too late. And yet she'd had time to linger over cobbler and cocoa with Colter. Had time to relax with Rebel, pet her soft fur and enjoy the dog's contagious happiness. Had time to look out Colter's big window at the amazing scenery below and just *be*.

Two days in Alaska and here she was, rethinking the choices she'd made in her life. But she'd always done what seemed right, from trying to look after her brother during those years her parents were lost in the search for Alanna to trying to make them proud of her. Trying to make up for letting Alanna get taken in the first place and keep her sister's legacy alive through music.

Would Alanna even like the violin today? Kensie had no way of knowing, but every time she picked up the instrument, she felt her sister's spirit. It kept Kensie connected to Alanna in a way nothing else could. But had she traded her own path for the things she thought would make her parents proud, keep their love strong after what she'd done? Had she traded a chance to really live her life for the whirlwind that kept her from thinking too much about what she'd lost and what she really wanted?

The idea made anxiety rise in her chest until she clutched a hand there. It actually physically hurt. And she suspected it was only a fraction of the pain Colter felt whenever he suddenly seemed overcome by memories.

She couldn't dwell on it very long because, up the street, a man who looked like he topped six feet, with gray-streaked brown hair and a heavy jean jacket, stepped out of a store. Her heart rate took off and she walked faster, wanting to get close without his spotting her. Could it be Henry Rollings?

He headed away from her, walking with long strides, but not seeming to realize she was behind him. *It was him.* Okay, she wasn't positive, but she was pretty sure. It was the same jacket she'd seen earlier, the same dark hair, shot through with gray.

Swallowing back her nerves, Kensie glanced behind her as Henry turned the corner up ahead. Where was he going? And where was Colter? If Henry really was connected to her sister's disappearance, she wasn't sure she wanted to face him alone. An ex-Marine with a shotgun at her side seemed like a good idea about now.

She dug in her pocket for her cell phone to text Colter just as Henry turned a corner. Scared of losing him, Kensie shifted from a fast walk to a jog. When she turned the corner after him, she slowed, stepping more carefully, softly. She didn't dare slip her phone out of her pocket now, afraid it would make too much noise. Even her breathing seemed too loud here.

There'd been a handful of people around on the last street, but this one was totally empty. The stores here were all dark, alleyways and parking lots dimly lit and quiet. Just the man she hoped was Henry Rollings striding along ahead of her. She had no idea where he was going. It didn't seem like there was anything here, unless his truck was down an alleyway or in one of the tiny lots peppering the small openings between some of the stores.

Had he spotted her reflection in a store window as she chased after him? Was he leading her into a trap?

Slowly, she slid her hand deeper into her pocket, bypassing her phone and groping instead for the key to her rental truck. It wasn't much of a weapon, but it was all she had. And there was no turning back now. Not if there was a chance he could lead her to Alanna.

She took another step and her right foot slid. Kensie pinwheeled her arms, trying to regain her balance as she realized there was slick ice underneath her.

Just as she caught traction again, the guy up

ahead glanced back. His eyes widened at the sight of her. It *was* Rollings!

He whipped his head forward again and took off running.

Kensie raced after him, her new boots unfamiliar and sliding on random patches of ice. He turned another corner and tears pricked her eyes as she finally made it around the same spot.

He was gone.

She glanced both ways, desperately searching for a glimpse of him or any hint of where he could have gone. One way led to another alley and maybe back to the main part of town. The other led off into a group of freestanding storage units. And walking into those storage units, was that…?

Kensie craned her head forward, squinting into the darkness. A woman with dark, shoulder-length hair. Something familiar about the slope of her shoulders, the shape of her head. Was it even possible?

"Alanna!" Her sister's name erupted from her mouth in a desperate, high-pitched squeak, but the woman heard.

She glanced backward and Kensie almost fainted right there in the dark street.

After all these years, she'd actually done it. She'd found Alanna.

Chapter Ten

She'd just seen her sister. The realization stunned Kensie so much she froze. And then Alanna was gone, disappearing into the maze of storage units.

Why would she walk away? Where was she going?

It *was* Alanna. It didn't matter that Kensie hadn't seen her sister in fourteen years, that she'd grown from a young child to a woman in that time. It didn't matter that Kensie had only gotten a brief, unexpected look at her face before she'd turned away.

It was *her*. Kensie knew it down deep in her soul, in the space that had been empty since her sister was taken. In the space that had burned with hope and determination, an unwillingness to let Alanna go, ever since.

Sucking in a deep breath as she realized she'd actually stopped breathing, Kensie stepped forward again and a glint of light in the store window she was passing caught her eye. A reflection from behind her. A person's reflection, moving stealthily toward her.

Kensie stared at it from the corner of her eye, not turning her head at all, not wanting to let whoever it was know she'd seen him. A jolt shot through her, leaving panic behind, as she figured out who it was. The guy who'd told her he was ex-military, who'd tried to lure her into his truck. Danny Weston.

Colter had called him dangerous, warned her to stay far away from him. Colter had been so certain Danny was a threat that he'd agreed to help her just to keep her away from the guy. Fear made her overheated inside her warm new winter clothes, but she tried to stay calm.

She could run from Danny, but could she actually *outrun* him? Her best bet would be to go down the alley, toward the main part of town. Toward help.

But if she went that way, she'd be going in the opposite direction from where her sister had disappeared. She'd lose Alanna again. And after fourteen desperate, painful years of searching, she couldn't risk it. So running wasn't an option.

Instead, she fumbled inside her coat pocket again, this time for her cell phone. Would Danny react if he saw her using it, come after her sooner instead of just tracking her? Assuming following her somewhere and then hurting her was his intent. Maybe he was just walking around.

But that was wishful thinking and she knew it. There was no one else here. All the stores were closed. And Danny had already tried to lure her off with him once.

He'd failed. And she might not know Danny, but years of working with other families dealing with their own cold cases had taught her about people like him. Failure was a hit to his ego. He'd try again. It wasn't inevitable it would be with her, but she'd offered him an opportunity tonight. And she was pretty sure he'd try to take it.

Kensie pulled her cell phone out slowly, carefully, keeping it low in front of her body where he wouldn't see it. Thank goodness Colter had programmed his number in at his cabin.

She couldn't risk a phone call. So she typed out a frantic text, her hands shaking, praying she was giving him an accurate sense of where she was right now. Praying Colter could get to his truck, grab his shotgun and then get over here fast enough to help her.

She was a strong and capable woman, trained in basic self-defense, but Danny Weston was a lot bigger. In any other circumstances, she'd do the logical thing and run for help, screaming the entire way.

But logic didn't get a say when her sister was involved. Right now, Kensie could only think with her heart.

So, as she hit Send on her message to Colter,

she kept moving. Toward those dark storage units. Toward Alanna.

As she did, a new reason to panic occurred to her. Could Danny and Henry be working together? Maybe they were luring her out here to grab her. Might she have found Alanna only to disappear with her?

Her parents might survive losing another child. Unlike a lot of families who'd gone through this experience, they'd banded together instead of being slowly ripped apart. The divorce rate was astronomical for parents who lost a child. But her parents had made it, in some ways seeming closer now than they had before Alanna went missing.

But what about her brother, Flynn? He'd already gotten so out of control at sixteen that he'd almost died while driving drunk one night, another dangerous stunt, probably crying for attention, for help. Yeah, he was much better now. But he relied on her regular check-ins, relied on a support group still. This might set him back so far it would destroy him.

Her chest hurt at the idea of choosing between Alanna and Flynn. She loved both of them. She was the oldest and although she'd failed Alanna, she'd always seen it as her job to look after them.

But did she really have a choice right now? She'd let Colter know where she was. Hopefully he'd see the text and come in time. If she turned or ran, Danny would know she'd seen him. And

Henry had already spotted her following him, so would he stick around if she didn't catch up to him now? Or would he take Alanna and disappear somewhere else? Somewhere they'd never find her again?

Fear burned in Kensie's chest, the cold searing her lungs as she took too-fast breaths. She stepped off the sidewalk, crossed the snow-covered dirt road and stepped between storage units. Without store windows to show her Danny's reflection, she relied on her ears, listening carefully for footfalls. But the snow muffled most of them except for the occasional squish of a heavy boot in a slushy spot or the slight rustle of his clothing. Her phone was clutched tightly in her hand, but the screen stayed dark. Had Colter even seen her message?

The sun was sinking fast, casting beautiful reds and oranges across the sky, but the light didn't reach well between the storage units. It did a better job of casting shadows than providing light. Why would Henry even come back here?

She was an idiot. This had to be a trap. There was nothing here except plenty of places to hide between units and jump out at her when she was least expecting it.

Just as she was considering how to turn around without running into Danny, she realized where Henry and Alanna must have been going. Beyond the storage units was more parking. It looked empty, but she could only see a sliver of the lot, so she had to assume Henry had parked there. Maybe to keep Alanna out of sight while he shopped? Had she sneaked out of his truck, looking for help? But if she had, why had she kept walking when Kensie called her?

Kensie would figure that out when she found her. Glancing one last time at her cell phone, Kensie tucked it into her pocket and picked up her pace. She hadn't spotted Henry once since she'd started down this trail and for all she knew, he'd turned a different way.

But as she emerged from the storage units into a parking lot, she saw a black truck firing to life. And in the passenger seat was a woman with dark, shoulder-length hair.

No! The cry stuck in Kensie's throat. Without knowing what she was going to do, Kensie took off running, straight for the truck. Instead of trying to stand behind it—and probably getting run over for her trouble—she redirected toward the passenger side.

The truck was starting to back out, but slowly, like the driver hadn't spotted her. She could reach it! If the door was unlocked, Kensie could rip it open and pull Alanna out.

She was so close! A few more steps and her sister would be free. Then the driver's head tilted upward, like he was looking in his rearview, and the truck raced backward. It slammed to a stop—

presumably as he shifted into Drive. But that was all the time Kensie would need.

She stretched her hand out toward the door handle, toward Alanna. Then an arm wrapped around her ribs from behind and a hand slapped over her mouth. Someone bigger and taller wrenched her off her feet, smothering her scream as the truck roared out of the lot, taking Alanna with it.

WHERE WAS KENSIE?

Colter hadn't seen her in over an hour. He'd finished talking to the occupants of the bar twenty minutes ago, expecting to find her waiting by his truck. Although the stores were spread out, there wasn't a whole lot still open. Soon it would just be the bar.

He'd checked his cell phone, but nothing. So, then he'd started moving, peeking down most of the side streets, even popping into the few stores not yet closed. But no Kensie.

Nerves settled low in his belly, along with guilt that he'd let her wander around alone. Except she should have been perfectly safe here. Yes, it was quiet, but as far as he knew, the only trouble they'd ever had originated in the bar. Usually fights, which was why he'd suggested Kensie check the stores.

But there wasn't a lot to check, so why wasn't she back yet? And if she'd found anything, why hadn't she called? Yes, cell service could be spotty here, but it was usually okay as long as she stayed on the main streets.

Now, as the colorful streaks in the sky sank lower behind the trees, Colter glanced at Rebel. She'd sat patiently outside the bar waiting for him. He should have sent her with Kensie.

Rebel let out a low whine, as if she knew what he was thinking and agreed.

"Come on, girl, let's find Kensie," he said, picking up his pace even as his bad leg throbbed in protest.

Her tail wagged, but she watched him, as if he should know where she was. Which he should.

"Where are you, Kensie?" he asked out loud, making the woman closing up shop nearby glance at him sideways.

"Have you seen a woman with long brown hair and a purple coat come through here? She would have been looking for—"

"Her sister." The woman cut him off. "Yeah, I saw her about five minutes ago."

His heart picked up. Five minutes wasn't very long. And there wasn't much else down this street besides a few other shops, already closed up for the night, a couple of small parking lots and a group of storage units. Maybe she'd looped the long way around back to town and they'd just missed each other. "Do you know which way she headed?"

The woman silently pointed down the street—

toward the storage units—and then rounded the corner into the tiny parking lot next to her store.

Colter opened his mouth to ask if she was sure, but she'd seemed certain. He frowned, walking that way, but glancing down every alleyway he passed. A flash of movement caught his eye up ahead, and then a truck careened out from the side alongside the storage units. And in the passenger seat...was that Kensie?

"Kensie!" Her name ripped from his mouth as the truck did a dangerously sharp turn onto the street across from him. It would be gone long before he could get back to his truck and follow.

Panic and dread and loss filled him instantly, completely. They overwhelmed him, made his vision go dark like it had that day he'd learned about his brothers in the hospital. He slumped down into a crouch. His leg nearly gave out on him, but he managed to catch himself, resting his head on his knees, trying to get air into his suddenly uncooperative windpipe.

Beside him, Rebel let out a sharp bark and jabbed her head under his armpit. She nudged him with her nose over and over, grounding him, slowly settling the ringing in his ears.

And then he heard it. Kensie. A muffled shout of his name.

Was he hallucinating? He glanced at Rebel, who jerked to attention, straining forward without moving her feet.

It hadn't been Kensie in the truck. His hands shook so hard he could barely push himself back to a standing position, but he gritted his teeth and tried to get it together. Because from the sound of her voice, Kensie was in trouble.

He ran between the towering storage units, glancing back and forth, checking for threats far less effectively than he'd been trained. But Kensie's voice had come from the far side of the units; he was almost positive.

Rebel raced at his side, capable of outrunning him, but a loyal partner even now that they were both retired. She understood the Marines' code as well as he did; she'd never leave him.

"Good girl," he told her, pushing his leg even harder. Tiny knives danced up his thigh and he gritted his teeth, desperate to get to Kensie. Up ahead, he heard scuffling sounds, but nothing else.

Finally, the storage units ended and he shot out into a dark, dingy parking lot he hadn't even known was back here. At the far end of it was a dumpster. And Kensie, being dragged toward it by Danny Weston.

He had one arm manacled around her waist. The other hand was over her mouth, with his thumb jammed under her chin. Probably to keep her from screaming again. Or maybe she'd bitten him. He hoped she'd bitten him.

"Weston!" Colter barked, putting every ounce of command he could into it.

The man started, his gaze jolting upward as Colter ran straight at him, Rebel still at his side.

Right before they reached him, Danny swung Kensie violently sideways. She flew out of his grasp, slamming into the dumpster with a sickening, metallic thud.

"Kensie!" He stared at her, desperate to see movement, seeking out blood.

Before he could determine if she was okay, Danny was rushing him, ducking his head low and coming at him like a linebacker.

But Colter had been a Marine. He darted left, flicking his hand at Rebel in a silent command to go right.

She obeyed and Danny didn't adjust in time, flying between them. Colter spun, wincing at the trembling in his knee, but still ready to pound Danny into the ground.

But the jerk was faster than Colter had expected, already facing him, already realizing his weakness. Before Colter could react, Danny kicked out hard with a steel-toed boot, slamming into Colter's damaged leg, right above the knee.

Colter hit the pavement hard, face-first. Pain erupted in his head and thigh, and a million spots of light danced in front of his eyes until he thought he might throw up.

But Kensie was still in danger if he passed out,

so Colter mustered up everything he had and flipped to his back.

Just in time to see that Danny had grabbed a pipe and was swinging it toward his head.

Chapter Eleven

The growl that emerged from Rebel's mouth in that moment was unlike anything Colter had ever heard.

Danny froze, pipe in midair, and then shifted, swinging that deadly metal at Rebel.

Colter knew he'd never get to his feet fast enough to stop it. There was only one option and it was going to hurt like crazy. He swung his bad leg as hard as he could into Danny's knees, knocking the man sideways.

Pain jolted up his leg to his head, then raced back down, until he couldn't tell what was damaged and what wasn't. But Danny toppled to his knees, dropping the pipe.

Then Rebel leaped on him, knocking him the rest of the way down. She wasn't an attack dog, but she was strong and Colter knew she'd do anything to protect him.

But he wasn't going to let her get hurt for him. Not again.

Colter wasn't sure he could stand, so he rolled

sideways toward Danny, slamming a fist into the man's groin. He didn't like to fight dirty, but Rebel's life was at stake. So was Kensie's.

Danny yelped and curled inward, making Rebel jump off him. But it wasn't enough. And Colter wasn't going to win this battle from the ground. He needed to get up.

Danny was recovering faster than Colter, already rolling to his side and getting leverage to push to his feet. If Danny stood first, it was game over.

So Colter clamped his jaw against the pain and put his palms to pavement. With everything he had, he pushed upward, shoving himself to his feet.

It still wasn't going to be enough. Through eyes watering from pain, he could see Danny readying himself to deliver a knockout punch, fueled by rage and embarrassment and a dark soul.

His gaze jumped over to Kensie at the same time Colter's did. Somehow, while they'd been on the ground, she'd risen and crept up on them.

Time seemed to move in slow motion as Danny's eyes widened and he tried to swivel toward Kensie. But he was too slow.

Her punch was well aimed, despite the slight wobble as she pivoted toward him. It didn't take Danny down, but it knocked him back several steps and he shook his head, clearly seeing stars.

Colter didn't hesitate. He didn't know how long

he could stand, but he had one last push in him. And it didn't matter if he collapsed as long as he took Danny down hard with him. He raced at Danny, ducking his head like Danny had done initially. But Colter made contact, slamming into him hard enough to make Danny buckle and send them both back to the pavement.

Danny landed beneath him, head smacking the concrete with an echoing bang. His eyes blinked open and closed and his arms drooped. Then his eyes popped open again and he shoved at Colter. But his strength was diminished enough that Colter had no trouble holding him down.

Then sirens were screaming toward him. Soon, someone was lifting him to his feet and rolling Danny over, slapping on handcuffs as Kensie talked a mile a minute to another officer.

Colter recognized both officers, and by how quickly they'd realized Danny was the aggressor, he figured they'd recognized him, too. He nodded his thanks as one of them explained, "We got a call from a store owner about a woman yelling for help."

The officer let go of his arm and Colter's whole right side seemed to collapse. He would have fallen if Kensie hadn't darted over to support him, slipping her smaller body beneath his shoulder. Still, the force of his knee giving out almost took them both down.

Colter fought it, shifting as much weight as he

could onto his left leg. His right one screamed in agony and even without having to bear weight, it shook uncontrollably.

"You okay? You need an ambulance?" the officer asked as his partner dragged Danny away.

Danny screamed obscenities and threats the entire way to being shoved into the back of the police cruiser. The officer who'd helped him up didn't even glance his partner's way, apparently assuming she had it under control as he continued to stare at Colter with concern.

"I'm all right," Colter said, as Rebel let out a dissenting whine.

"You need to go to the hospital," Kensie insisted.

"I know my injury. It just needs rest." Colter hoped he was right. "But what about you? You hit that dumpster hard. You were unconscious. I want a doctor to look at you."

"I'm fine." Kensie sighed, frowning down at his leg.

"Ambulance is right around the corner," the officer said. "We'll have them look at both of you and the paramedics can decide."

"But—" Kensie started.

"Let's go," the officer said, his tone brooking no argument.

Rebel barked her agreement.

DRIVING COLTER'S TRUCK made her nervous. It was a big, hulking beast, capable of handling the steep drive up to his cabin, but taking up more of the road than she was used to managing.

The man next to her made Kensie nervous, too. He looked like he belonged on a Marine recruitment poster, with his well-defined muscles and intense blue eyes. He'd gritted his teeth while the medic poked and examined his leg and suggested he get an X-ray to make sure all the metal holding his thigh together was still intact. Then he'd calmly shaken his head and limped to the truck.

But he'd been in no shape to drive and they both knew it. So Kensie had gotten behind the wheel, after being cleared by the medic as having no obvious signs of concussion. Still, since she'd been briefly unconscious, they'd warned her to go to the hospital herself if she experienced any dizziness, vomiting or confusion.

Right now there was definite confusion, but it had nothing to do with Danny Weston throwing her against that disgusting dumpster. She risked another glance at Colter out of the corner of her eye. He looked terrible, his face so pale that she knew he was in a lot of pain. But he hadn't complained once. And she wasn't sure how to help him without hurting his pride.

Rebel looked just as worried as Kensie parked Colter's truck outside his cabin. She'd barely stepped out of the vehicle before the dog leaped over the front seat and climbed out after her. Rebel ran around to the passenger side faster than Kensie, but Colter had already gotten his door open and was trying to swivel himself out of the truck without bending his leg.

Kensie wedged herself in the door opening, sliding her arm behind his back and bracing herself for his weight. "Lean on me."

"I've got it," he said, sounding more frustrated than harsh.

"Yeah, I know, but this will be easier," she said, trying to sound cheerful. But she couldn't quite manage it. Residual fear still clung to her from her encounter with Danny. Fear about what could have happened to her. Fear about what had almost happened to Rebel and Colter.

His eyes narrowed on her, as if he could read her thoughts, and then he did lean on her just a little as he hauled himself out of the truck. The step down to the ground was shaky and Kensie did her best to absorb the impact, but she could still tell he was hurting.

It took them several minutes to make the short trek to the cabin door, with Rebel running circles around them most of the way.

"Rebel, chill," Colter finally said, a smile cracking through as she plopped down on her butt.

"She loves you," Kensie said as he fumbled with the key and got the door open.

"Yeah, well, I love her, too," Colter replied, bracing himself on the doorjamb to take some of his weight off her. "We saw three years of combat together. We train as partners and that's what she is. I'd take a bullet for her and she almost took one for me."

Kensie glanced back at Rebel, who was waiting patiently for Colter to make it through the doorway before she followed. "You saved her today."

"She saved me in Afghanistan," he answered simply, pulling away from her a little to peel his coat off and drop it on the floor.

"You saved me today, too." Her text had never gone through, but he'd come for her anyway, taking on Danny despite his own injuries.

Colter glanced at her briefly before continuing a slow walk toward his recliner. "We saved each other."

His words were filled with so many emotions. Honesty and admiration, yes, but also embarrassment. Probably because he hadn't been able to take Danny down on his own. But it wasn't a fair fight when Colter had a damaged leg.

She knew saying that would only fuel Colter's resentment and frustration at his situation. Instead, she stayed silent, helping him lower himself into his recliner.

Once seated, he sighed and rested his head back against the chair, closing his eyes. It gave her the chance to stare at him, at the very faint lines on his forehead, the thick blond-tinged eyebrows, down over a strong nose to strong, full lips. Lips she'd tasted more than once. Lips she wanted to taste again right now.

His eyes flicked open. There was heat in his gaze, but amusement in the tilt of his lips. "You mind shutting the door, Kensie? It's cold in here."

She hurried toward the door, feeling a flush shoot up her face. Although what reason did she have to be embarrassed? They'd already kissed twice. He knew she was attracted to him. She faltered as she pushed the heavy cabin door shut. But did he know that what he'd done had drawn her to him even more?

He deserved to know that. He deserved to know that while he was sitting there, obviously feeling like a failure for not taking down Danny Weston all alone, in her mind, doing it despite his injury made Colter more heroic.

"What are you thinking?" Colter asked softly, making her realize she'd been standing there too long without turning back. "If you think you're up for it, you can head back to your hotel. I don't mind if you take my truck."

"That's not…" She turned to face him, clutching her hands together. To make sure he knew she had no intention of leaving, she tossed her coat and yanked off her boots. "I know, being a Marine, you're used to being able to take on any threat all by yourself."

"Not really." He cut her off, looking uncomfortable. "Marines work in units. I mean, yeah,

I was an MP and a K-9 handler, which is a little different. But I still had a partner." He glanced at Rebel, whose tail swung back and forth as she glanced between them.

"I don't know what you're thinking right now," she continued, even though she was pretty sure she *did* know. It was in the slump of his shoulders, the downturn of his lips, the way he'd hung his head as he'd told the officers what happened. He felt like less of a man.

Well, screw that. She walked slowly toward him, forcing herself to keep eye contact even though the strength of his gaze made her too warm inside. Made it hard to concentrate on her words.

But she tried, because she owed him that much after what he'd done for her. And not just in that parking lot, but every moment since she'd met him. "Having an injury doesn't make you less."

He blew out a loud breath through his nose, like he disagreed, but she didn't give him time to cut her off.

"You could have used that as an excuse. Not just today, but for everything I've asked you to do. But you haven't." She kept approaching, her tone gaining conviction with every word, because it was all true. "You acted anyway. You put yourself in harm's way to help me and Rebel." Her voice broke as she reached the side of his chair and took his hand. "You're the most incredible man I've ever met."

She hadn't realized she thought it until the words came out, but they were true. No one had ever put so much on the line for her, and she barely knew him. What must he be like when it was someone he loved?

He stared back at her, the expression on his face shifting from disbelief and self-disgust to contemplation to something soft and raw that made her legs feel weak. Then his fingers were sliding through hers, his touch making nerves all over her body fire to life.

On Colter's other side, Rebel let out a short bark, startling her and breaking the spell. But as soon as she turned her smiling gaze back to Colter, the feeling returned. Because he was still staring up at her with an intensity that said her words had penetrated. Maybe she'd even made him believe them.

She slid her palm over the scruff coming in on Colter's cheek, then leaned in. It was an awkward angle, but when his lips grazed hers, it didn't matter. Happiness filled her, instant and so powerful that it overwhelmed everything else. She pushed forward, pressing her mouth more tightly to his, and almost fell into his lap.

She caught herself on the recliner arm just in time. "Sorry," she breathed.

"Come here," he whispered back, tugging her toward him.

Carefully, she pivoted her body over the chair, so she was straddling him without putting any weight on him. Her knees were on either side of him, her butt arched awkwardly in the air, but it didn't matter, because now her hands could slip around his neck.

He stared at her a long moment, all of that intensity directed solely at her making her squirm. Then he cupped her face with his big palm, drawing her closer until her lips settled on his again. He kissed her softly at first, the merest grazing of his lips and tongue against hers that left her whole body aching for more. When she couldn't take another moment of the slow torture, she fisted a hand in the front of his shirt and picked up the tempo until her head started spinning.

Colter's kisses grew deeper, more demanding, until everything else in the world ceased to exist. Slowly, she became aware of his hands slipping underneath the back of her shirt, his long fingers caressing their way up her back. She'd been content with just kissing him; knowing the way his leg was, he wasn't up for more. But suddenly she craved the feel of his skin against hers.

Her hands shook as they felt their way down impressive pecs and a muscled torso. Then she grabbed a fistful of his T-shirt and pulled up-

ward. He leaned forward and helped her pull it
over his head.

She'd planned to peel off her own shirt next, but
got distracted by the expanse of bare skin in front
of her. Drinking the sight in, her gaze stalled on
his left biceps. Script circled his arm and as she
traced the words, the muscles there leapt under
her fingertips. "Semper Fi," she read aloud, her
voice husky.

"Latin," he told her, his beautiful blue eyes
fixed on hers even as his hands returned to their
trek over her rib cage. "The Marines' motto. It
means always faithful."

Loyalty. A smile trembled on Kensie's lips as
her body responded to his touch, arching forward.
Of course. A man like Colter lived by those words.
He was loyal to Rebel, loyal to the memory of
his lost brothers, even loyal to the promise he'd
made her.

And right now, she wanted to show him how
much she appreciated it. She leaned back in.

"I'm so glad you're not hurt," he whispered
against her lips.

She jerked back, a jolt of realization and hor-
ror slicing through her. She'd been so distracted
by Colter—by his reinjuring his leg, by her feelings for him—that she'd forgotten to tell him what
she'd discovered.

With tears pricking her eyes, she scrambled off him. "Colter, I found her."

"What?"

"I think I found Alanna."

Chapter Twelve

Kensie's words filtered slowly through Colter's haze of desire. "You *what*?"

"I think I found her, Colter." She crossed her arms over her chest, pacing in front of him.

Rebel stood near the bottom of his recliner, her ears perked, head swiveling to follow Kensie's frantic movements.

"Okay." Colter leaned forward, then grimaced as pain jolted up his thigh. It had faded into the background with Kensie's soft lips on his, her skin beneath his fingers. Now it was back, full force. Swallowing nausea, he studied her.

A minute ago, she'd been fire and energy in his lap. Now, she was all nervous agitation and desperate hope. "Tell me what happened."

"It's that guy. The one I saw in the snowplow store."

"Henry Rollings?"

"Yeah. I followed him toward the end of the shops and then he turned a corner and I lost him. I was trying to decide which way he'd gone when

I saw Alanna heading into the area with the storage units."

Colter absorbed her words more slowly than he would have liked, still a little distracted by the swollen pinkness of her lips, the rapid rise and fall of her chest. By the memory imprinted on his mind of her climbing on top of him, of the touch of her fingertips still searing his skin. "Why would she go back there? Was he dragging her?"

"No." Kensie stopped moving, her shoulders slumping, lines knitting her forehead. "She just walked in. It was after I'd lost him. I was trying to decide his most likely route when I spotted her."

Rebel moved as soon as Kensie stopped, hurrying over and shoving her nose under Kensie's hand. Without seeming to realize it, Kensie started petting Rebel, who sat and made herself comfortable.

"So, you followed this woman you think is Alanna?" Colter clarified. "Not Henry?"

Her head jerked back slightly. "Well, yeah, I guess so. I just assumed he went that way, too, once I saw her."

"And what about Danny? Was he with her?"

"No, Danny was following me."

Colter held back the slew of questions that bubbled up. When had she spotted Danny following her? Why had she gone into a deserted location if she'd known Danny was on her trail?

Colter didn't ask because he knew the answer. Her sister.

Kensie's lips folded upward, contrition in her gaze as her hand went still on Rebel's head. "I had to try and get to her, Colter."

"I understand." And he did. He didn't blame her for it, either, no matter the state of his leg. "But what would you have done if you'd caught up to her? If she was really walking that way without being forced…"

The thought trailed off as he realized that the truck that had flown past him moments before he'd heard Kensie's scream—the one he'd thought carried Kensie away from him—must have held Alanna. He'd been devastated, thinking it was Kensie being ripped out of his life. So how must Kensie feel, knowing it was the sister she'd been searching for since she was thirteen?

"Are you sure it was her?" He had to ask, even though he couldn't deny the resemblance. But then, he'd only gotten a brief glimpse of the woman in the truck's passenger seat. Dark hair, similar profile. He'd just assumed, because he knew Kensie had gone in that direction.

Maybe Kensie was just assuming, too, because she wanted so desperately for it to be Alanna.

The woman he'd seen hadn't been tied down in the back, out of sight. She'd been sitting up in the passenger seat as if she was there of her own free will. None of that sounded like a woman who'd been kidnapped.

"I-it had to be her," Kensie said. He must have looked unconvinced, because she started petting Rebel again, faster, as she rushed on. "I yelled her name. She turned toward me when she heard it, Colter. It was her. It was Alanna."

"Are you sure? Then why did she keep going? Maybe she just turned because you startled her, Kensie." He didn't want to destroy her hope, but he had to ask.

"Long-term kidnapping victims bond to their captors," Kensie told him haltingly, like she didn't want to know about such things, let alone talk about them. "They do it just to survive. Someone like Alanna, grabbed when she was only five…" She broke off on a sob that she quickly stifled. "It's possible she doesn't even know she was kidnapped, that she doesn't remember her family. That she doesn't remember me."

"I'm sorry." He cursed himself for not thinking it through. It made sense. Long-term prisoners of war sometimes did the same thing.

Not wanting Kensie to dwell on what her sister might have endured over all those years, he turned the conversation in another direction. "Are you sure she was with Henry? Did you ever see them together?"

Kensie squinted up at the ceiling, like she was trying to recall, then finally shook her head. "No,

I can't be positive. I assume it was him driving the truck I saw her in, but I couldn't actually see the driver. But what are the chances he led me that way and then Alanna just happened to be there? Especially after he ran from me at the snowplow store when I started asking questions?"

Unless he was trying to lead Kensie to her sister. Trying to lure her into a trap she couldn't resist and then grab her, too. But Danny Weston had almost beaten him to it. Colter kept the dark thoughts to himself.

He also didn't voice a more immediate concern. If Henry thought Kensie was following him around, if he knew she'd seen Alanna, would he disappear now?

He should suggest the possibility to Kensie, but he didn't want her running off trying to find Henry alone. Especially if Henry *had* hoped to take both sisters. Because, right now, Henry had a big advantage. He knew Kensie would do whatever it took to save Alanna. And they still had no real idea where to look for him.

Besides, no matter how much he wanted to be, Colter was in no shape to go anywhere right now. Not even to help Kensie. No matter how badly he wished he could.

"It had to be Henry, right?" Kensie pressed when he stayed quiet too long.

"Probably," Colter agreed, but his mind was

only half on Henry now. Because maybe they were both letting their hopes run wild.

Alanna had been missing for a long time. What was the likelihood Kensie had just spotted her walking around town, no matter how deserted it was? Especially after that note had shown up and drawn the FBI, making the townspeople more alert for a possible sighting of the missing woman? Would a kidnapper really let her out into public with that added scrutiny?

Kensie told him she was pretty sure she'd seen Alanna, but maybe that was just because she wanted it so badly. The FBI thought the note was a hoax. Maybe this wasn't real, either, just a woman who looked like Alanna might have after fourteen years of growing up.

Maybe the best thing he could do for Kensie wasn't to help her chase these potentially dangerous men, but to help her move on with her own life. Help her accept that Alanna was gone. Help her realize that her own life was still worth living, that she deserved to have her own future.

Except how could he do that when he didn't believe the same was true for himself?

THE WAY A person changed between the ages of five and nineteen was enormous. Colter had been right to ask if she could be sure the woman she'd seen was Alanna. The very idea that it might not be made Kensie's chest constrict and her brain want to shut down. She'd spent so long searching. She wasn't sure she could bear another dead end.

But this time really did feel different. She couldn't explain it, except that it had been years since she'd felt this surge of hope, this restrained happiness waiting to burst free. In the beginning, she'd experienced it often. But over the years, that had faded, leaving behind a hope that was much more jaded, much more cautious.

Since she'd first heard about the note in Desparre, though, something had taken hold of her, something deeper than desperation. She wanted to believe it was the bond she and Alanna had always shared, rearing up and screaming at her not to miss her chance to bring Alanna home.

"Kensie."

Colter's voice broke through her thoughts and she realized he was stretching his hand toward her. She stepped closer, threading her fingers through his and hanging on tight.

Rebel scooted forward, too, nudging up to Kensie's side the way she'd seen the dog do with Colter.

With the two of them beside her, Kensie's tension eased a little. Knowing she truly wasn't in this alone cleared the panic from her mind enough to strategize. "I think we should go to the police. They must be able to get an address for Henry Rollings."

"Not necessarily," Colter replied. "And they

don't really have a reason to give it to us even if they have it. But I have to be honest, Kensie. From what I've heard about this guy, I think he lives off the grid. No one in the bar could tell me quite where, even the longtime locals, which says he doesn't want anyone to know."

"Well, the police should at least be able to help us—"

"We don't have any evidence that he's done anything wrong," Colter reminded her. "We can't even be sure this woman was with him or that she's actually Alanna."

"But—"

"We can try the police if you want. I just don't want you to get your hopes up for their help. Look, a military investigation is different, so maybe I'm wrong or we'll get lucky. I'm just telling you what I know about the process. You've probably encountered it, too."

"Yeah." Evidence was king. Police generally weren't interested in the theories of civilians. It was fair, but frustrating.

She stared at Colter, and she couldn't stop her gaze from drifting to his bare chest. For a man who'd sustained a serious injury a year ago, he was in amazing shape. Running her hands over all of those muscles had made her giddy with lust. Her fingers twitched in his now, wanting a return visit.

Forcing her gaze back up, Kensie said, "I don't need the police. I know you can help me track Rollings."

Colter's lips pressed together into a hard line. "I'm going to do my best, Kensie, but tonight…" He sighed heavily.

"I know. It's okay. We should wait for the light anyway, and honestly, I'm still a little shaken up from earlier."

It was true. If she let herself think too long about how close she'd come to being Danny Weston's prey—for whatever terrible thing he had planned for her—she'd lose it. Only Colter's kisses and his soft touch had swept away the lingering feel of Danny's aggressive, sweaty hands.

Still, the words were hard to say, because the truth was that she wanted to rush back out now. She was terrified that since Henry had spotted her following him, he'd skip town for good and take Alanna with him. But Kensie also had fourteen years of practice watching how investigations worked. Right now, she had no clue where to find Henry. And she'd learned her lesson about going after him alone.

She needed Colter. And she needed him uninjured. "Are you sure you don't want to go to the hospital?"

"I know my injury, Kensie. It probably seems like I'm being a typical boneheaded man, but I've lived with this for the past year. It hurts pretty bad right now, but it's nothing compared to what it was like even six months ago. It'll heal. It'll suck in the meantime, but it'll heal. I need elevation, ice and rest."

She peeled her hand free and hurried into the attached kitchen to get him some ice. "How much rest?" It was insensitive, but as much as she wanted Colter's help, time mattered right now. If he was going to be out of commission for a week, she'd have to find someone else to assist her.

The idea of having anyone else by her side while she searched for Alanna made anxiety gnaw away at her. Somehow, in two days, Colter and Rebel had managed to become much more than just local help. Much more than tools in the search for her sister. They'd become her friends, her support system.

She faltered, a bag full of ice in her hands. Colter had done so much for her, and when he'd said he should be dead alongside his brothers, words had failed her. Just like she'd failed him in that moment.

"Kensie?" Colter called. "What's wrong?"

How could he read her so well already? She'd never been someone who wore her feelings all over her face. Slamming the freezer door shut, she strode over to him and carefully placed the ice on his thigh.

Colter flinched at the contact, but didn't make a sound, except to say, "Thanks."

There was another chair on the opposite side of the room, but Kensie didn't want to be that far away when she broached the topic of his lost friends. So she perched on the edge of the hearth, her heart pounding frantically.

Since she'd gotten involved with groups chasing cold cases, she'd met a lot of families of victims. Some had gotten the worst possible news during the time she'd known them. When she could, she'd tried to support them, all the while praying she'd never be one of them. But she'd learned quickly that what helped one person hurt another. And she didn't want to hurt Colter. He'd faced too much pain already.

"Colter..."

He turned toward her, his beautiful blue eyes narrowing like he knew what was coming. Rebel rose from her spot on the other side of his recliner and ran around, plopping down between them. Ears perked, chin up, she stared at Colter like she was waiting for him to say something.

Kensie spoke first. "I like the picture in your room. The one where you have Rebel on your shoulders."

At her name, the dog's head swiveled toward Kensie, her tail wagging.

A short burst of laughter, half amusement at Rebel and half nervousness about the conversation, broke free. "Those were your brothers with you, right? Your Marine brothers?"

The picture had been perched sideways on his nightstand, as though sometimes he wanted to see it and others he turned it away from him. The photo showed everyone covered in dust, looking exhausted, and she'd wondered if they'd just returned from a mission, wondered what they'd been doing. Colter was in the middle, Rebel's front legs dangling over one shoulder and her back legs dangling over the other, with Colter holding both. Her tongue had been lolling out, her eyes a little droopy, like she was just as tired as the soldiers. But they'd all been smiling. Even Rebel's mouth was stretched outward, like she was happy, too.

"Kensie, you've seen what happens when I even think about that day." His voice grew quiet, like he hated admitting it. "I break down. I can't function. I don't want to talk about—"

"You don't have to tell me how they died, Colter. I want to know how they lived. You loved them, right?"

"Yeah."

"And they loved you."

It wasn't a question, but he nodded anyway.

"Don't you think they'd want—"

"Me to live?" Colter interrupted with a humorless laugh. "You think psychiatrists haven't played this game with me, Kensie?"

"It's not a ga—"

"It's not about that. Of course they'd want me to live. We all lived and breathed by the same code.

Loyalty. We did everything together. And maybe that's half the point. They all had families at home waiting for them. Every single one of them. Except me." He leaned forward, pain all over his face—but from his wound or his memories, she wasn't sure. "How is that fair?"

"It's not fair," she answered softly. "But you deserve a chance at happiness, too. You deserve a family."

As she spoke the words, she could actually imagine a family for him. A little boy with Colter's sky-blue eyes. Twin girls with Colter's slow grin and her own dark hair. Rebel chasing after all of them in a yard behind a cheerful yellow house. She and Colter watching, holding hands and laughing.

Kensie swayed backward at the intensity of her fantasy, at how *real* it felt, how possible. But it wasn't. Not even close. Her time with Colter was temporary.

Colter said something, but the words didn't process over the roaring crescendo of her heartbeat in her ears. Somehow, over the course of two days, she'd done more than just develop a silly crush on Colter.

She'd gone and fallen halfway in love with him.

Chapter Thirteen

She was falling in love with Colter Hayes. A man she barely knew.

It was ridiculous. It shouldn't even be possible. And yet, her heart thumping madly and her face flushing with the fear he might read her feelings in her eyes told her it was true.

"Kensie."

The way Colter said her name suggested he'd been repeating it. She jerked her gaze up to his, seeing the mix of confusion and concern.

His hands were braced on the recliner, all the distracting muscles in his arms outlined. "You swayed backward like you lost your balance. I think it might be from hitting your head. Maybe we need to get *you* to the hospital, get you an MRI."

How did she explain what had just happened without admitting her newly realized feelings? A burst of nervous laughter escaped.

Colter shoved himself forward, sliding down the recliner. At the motion, his jaw clamped so tightly that his lips turned inward and moisture filled the corners of his eyes. "What's going on? You need a doctor to check you out."

Jumping to her feet, Kensie held up a hand. "Stop! Don't move. I'm fine. I promise. I was just thinking about something and it surprised me. I feel normal, no headache, nothing. I don't have a concussion." She stood on one foot and pivoted in a circle. "See? My balance is fine."

He froze halfway down the recliner, eyes narrowed. "What were you thinking about?"

What could she tell him that was believable but wouldn't scare him into suggesting she find someone else to help her? Someone she wouldn't fall for after just a few days?

"Um…"

"Kensie." This time her name was filled with warning, like he already didn't believe her.

"I think I've spent most of my adult life trying to make up for letting Alanna get kidnapped." The words that burst from her mouth surprised her. Not the fact that she thought it; she'd realized it while she'd been wandering around town, searching for information on Henry. But it surprised her that she'd shared it.

Colter looked equally surprised. He stayed suspended halfway down the chair, his mouth open in a silent O.

Not wanting him to feel sorry for her—or think she didn't have a life—she backtracked. "I know it's not my fault. It's just survivor's guilt rearing up."

Great. Now she sounded like one of the psychiatrists her parents had insisted she see as a teenager.

"Of course it's not your fault."

Colter sounded almost offended by the idea, but he must have believed her, because his biceps bulged out again and then he hauled himself back up the chair. Leaning against the headrest, he closed his eyes, exhaustion in the slump of his shoulders and the way his chest heaved from the effort.

She hoped he'd drop the topic, but when his eyes opened again, they were soft, understanding.

"Why isn't your family here with you, Kensie? Helping you search for Alanna?"

It wasn't the question she'd expected him to ask and she felt herself flush for a new reason now. She didn't want him to think her family was mean or uncaring. "Because of what the FBI told us," she explained. "We've all been through this so many times over the years. There's been a lot of false leads. Once, two years after she was taken, we even drove down to Indiana to see a girl who'd been rescued. She wasn't talking and police thought it could be Alanna. It wasn't, but—"

That experience had scarred her. The girl had been a broken shell. Gaunt and terrified, and the same age as Alanna would have been then. Police had eventually found her family, but Kensie had kept track of her over the years. At thirteen she'd committed suicide.

"Anyway," Kensie rushed on, realizing she'd stopped talking long enough for concern to put lines across Colter's forehead. "My parents handled that one better than Flynn and I did."

"Of course they did. How old were you?"

"Fifteen."

Colter swore, and Kensie continued. "My parents did try hard to keep me and Flynn away from the search. But we wanted to know. We missed Alanna, too. We still do. And the longer Alanna was gone, the harder it was to get interest from the press, help from the public for tips. But they were a lot more interested if they could talk to me or Flynn."

"Oh, Kensie—"

"Flynn was younger than me, so I tried to do most of the press interviews. I thought I was protecting him, but it wasn't enough. It was never enough. My parents did their best for us, but they were trying to do their best for Alanna, too. And over the years, Flynn just got more and more out of control. Hanging out with a bad crowd, doing dangerous things just to cheat death or get some kind of rush—he's explained it to me, but I still don't totally understand."

Rebel let out a low whine and scooted closer, resting her head against Kensie's leg.

Kensie smiled at the dog, who seemed to have a finely tuned sense for when someone was hurting. Running her hand over Rebel's soft fur released a bit of the tension knotting Kensie's shoulders.

"When he was sixteen, he drove his car off a bridge. Not intentionally," she added, thinking of the girl in Indiana. "He was drunk. Thank goodness no one else was hurt. Flynn spent a month in the hospital. And that changed everything."

"What do you mean?" Colter asked softly.

"We have close family friends who say it woke my parents up to the fact that they had two other kids who needed them." When Colter frowned, she told him, "I don't think they ever forgot. But it was hard growing up with Alanna's disappearance always overshadowing everything. My parents missed birthdays chasing possible sightings. Flynn and I probably spent too much of our childhood talking to police and being interviewed by reporters and talk-show hosts. I wanted to do it, but Flynn…" She shook her head.

"So, if Flynn was sixteen when this happened, how old were you?"

"Twenty."

"So there was no do-over on your childhood at that point."

Kensie shrugged, uncomfortable with the implication. "I love my parents. They love me. They tried to do what was best for all three of their kids.

I understand that. Heck, I pushed them hard not to stop. And when they did—"

"You took over," Colter said, his intense gaze never leaving her face.

She shrugged. "Yeah. My parents needed to focus on Flynn. But we couldn't just give up on Alanna. She's my baby sister."

"So, now you chase after these leads all by yourself, with no one to lean on?"

"It's not like that. My family is only a phone call away. And I can't expect them to drop everything every time I think there might be a chance."

"They dropped everything for your sister when you were a kid."

"That's not fair," Kensie said, but it lacked heat because she knew Colter was just trying to take her side. The problem was, there were no sides. There was just sadness. Her parents' way meant accepting Alanna was long dead, lost to them forever. Her way meant the possibility of an endless cycle of hope and heartbreak.

"You're right," Colter said. "I'm sorry. But you shouldn't have to do this alone."

"I'm not doing it alone," Kensie said softly, her hand still absently stroking Rebel's head. "I've got you."

And that had changed everything. She stared at him, the soft understanding in his gaze, the ice hanging sideways off his leg, dripping unnoticed onto the chair.

She'd never met anyone like Colter Hayes. She'd probably never meet anyone like him again.

If this was what being halfway in love with him was like, she was in trouble. Because it would be far too easy to fall the rest of the way.

And she had a feeling if that happened, she'd never recover from the hard landing.

"I'VE GOT YOU."

Kensie's words echoed in his head, the soft, shy certainty in her voice tugging at his heart. She deserved someone to stand next to her, to help shoulder her burden for more than just a few days or a week or however long she was going to be in Desparre.

That was something he could never give her. But he could support her while she was there.

And he could open up to her, the way she'd opened up to him.

The very idea made his lungs constrict too hard with each breath, made his skin burn with clammy heat despite the ice melting all over his leg. But he pushed the words out anyway, praying he wouldn't have a full-blown panic attack in front of her.

"When I woke up in the hospital, the doctors told me they weren't sure they could save my leg."

Kensie's back straightened at his change in conversation, her hand slowing on Rebel's head.

As if sensing he needed her now, his dog came to the recliner and dangled her head over the chair arm. She nudged at his elbow, encouraging him to pet her, and he laughed at her antics.

But his laughter faded fast. "Pretty quickly, though, it didn't even matter what happened with my leg, because they told me none of my brothers had made it out of that ambush. Rebel got out, but they weren't sure she was going to pull through."

He smothered the sob that lurched forward at the memory. He could almost smell the hospital's nauseating mix of bleach and sickness. Saying the words was a softer blow now than it had been then, but it still felt like someone had punched him right in the chest.

Kensie lurched forward. She gripped his shoulder, not impeding the quickening motion of his hand petting Rebel. "You don't need to talk about this, Colter."

"I do. I want to tell you." As he spoke, he realized it was true.

He hadn't talked about that day since it happened, refusing to get into any detail with the shrinks the military kept offering him. Refusing to go into detail with his parents, who wanted to help him, but just couldn't move past their own mix of fear and joy that *he* was alive to understand his depression.

"You know that picture in my room you liked?"

"Yeah." Her voice was soft, barely above a whisper. He could actually hear her swallow, waiting for him to continue.

"It's the last one I have of them. We weren't technically a team. I was Military Police, K-9 Unit. Rebel's role was pretty new to the military then. She'd been serving for three years as a Combat Tracker Dog. It meant the two of us were partners. Sometimes we'd go with a unit, other times we'd get dropped into a site by ourselves."

"Dropped?" Kensie asked, her hand absently rubbing his shoulder.

He wondered if she even knew she was doing it. "Yeah. Helicopter would take us in and we'd rope out together. Rebel would be attached to me and we'd be set down somewhere, usually out in front of a unit to check out a location. Rebel's job was to start at the site of an explosion or an ambush and then follow the trail back to the person who set it. She was good at it, too."

At the praise, Rebel's tail darted back and forth a few times. But it settled fast, either because she knew what he was talking about or she recognized the serious tone of his voice.

"Anyway, for almost a year, Rebel and I had been attached to a Marine Special Operations Team. The guys you saw in the picture in my room were that unit. We all bonded fast. That day—the day the picture was taken—we'd just come back from a mission. We thought we were finished for the day. We should have been finished for the day."

He blew out a breath, remembering the moment

the call had come that they were going back out. There'd been nothing out of the ordinary about it. They'd all had just enough time to get cleaned up, get comfortable. But that was the way of missions sometimes. You might not see any real action for weeks and then, all of a sudden, you'd barely get any rest.

That day they'd heard about a bomb going off, listened to the initial reports. One of his brothers had said he hoped they'd be the ones to check it out. They all knew Rebel's success rate. They believed she could find the bomber who'd taken the lives of what he'd later learned were twenty-six soldiers.

That moment in the command tent was the last time they'd all been together before heading out. He could picture the whole group, in a combination of fatigues and fresh T-shirts, looking exhausted, but with a seriousness that said they were ready to go.

He blinked the image of his brothers away and Kensie refocused in front of him. She waited patiently, quietly, her hand still on his shoulder.

"It was an IED—improvised explosive device. A strong one. Blew up a couple of transports. A lot of our people were killed. The area was dangerous and reports said there were no expected survivors, so the Special Operations Team I was assigned to was sent out. Their job was to clear it for a Medevac unit to come in—with the hope that reports were wrong and there'd be people left to save. Rebel and I were supposed to get a scent on the guy who'd set the bomb."

When they'd arrived, the scene had been terrible. The trucks had been caught in a remote pass, an area known to be dangerous because of the terrain. The trucks could go between the rocky hills or all the way around. Around meant losing a lot of time. Between meant making a tempting target for the snipers who were known to hide up in the hills if they got word of a transport coming through. But this had been the first time someone had tried an IED there.

"I admit, I was nervous about the call once we got details. I had a feeling we'd be tracking this bomber up into territory well controlled by insurgents. But Rebel and I were going to wait for the rest of our team to finish their work and come with us if we needed to. But we never got the chance."

The wreckage had still been smoldering when they'd trekked in, alert for snipers looking to finish off anyone trapped in what remained of the transport vehicles. But there'd been no one left to hurt, no one left to save.

The smell of smoke and fuel had been overwhelming, the craters much bigger than anyone had expected. He'd known from a single look that it was too late for anyone who'd been in those trucks.

His vision blurred over at the memory. He'd known most of those people, and just like that, they were gone. It hadn't been the first time. But in that moment he'd tried not to linger on the pain. He'd tried to hold on to the anger. That's what would push him forward into the rocky hills with Rebel, looking for the bomber.

"Rebel got a scent," he told Kensie, realizing that it was tears blurring his vision. He felt her soft fingertips swiping them away for him as he pressed on. "It's probably why we made it. We were out in front of the rest of the team. They'd already cleared the immediate area, but the hills above? All we could do was watch those. So, Rebel and I were the first targets."

"Targets?" Kensie's voice wobbled and her hand clamped harder on his shoulder.

"It was an ambush. Once the bomber took the trucks, the others waited up in the hills until we'd searched the place, called it in as clear. Then they fired. An L-shaped ambush. Seems like all the fire is coming from one spot, so you move, and then you realize it's there, too. Probably the plan had been to get soldiers and then the first responders. Which isn't exactly what we were, but a Special Operations Team is a pretty tempting target."

Colter couldn't believe it had been a year now. The official after-action reports estimated that it had taken less than three minutes for everyone else on his team to be killed. And he'd missed all of it, hadn't been able to take a stand alongside them, because he'd already been out of the fight. It was one of the biggest regrets of his life.

The cabin was so silent he could hear Rebel's soft breathing, Kensie's more uneven breaths.

"How did you survive?" Kensie finally asked. Her voice was shaky and something wet dropped onto his arm that he realized was her tears.

"Rebel. That first shot was fired and she leaped on me. Kind of like she did with you the day we met you." He'd actually felt the next bullet slice right over his head, but by then he'd already been falling.

Rebel whined at the sound of her name, pressing her head against him, maybe recognizing he was moving into dangerous territory.

"It's okay, girl," he told her. Because it was. He'd already gotten through most of the story and he hadn't broken down.

Colter stared up at Kensie. Her lips trembled despite how hard she'd pressed them together. She was blinking rapidly, trying to contain the moisture covering her beautiful toffee-colored eyes.

She cared about him. The thought filled him with joy and pride and fear. He didn't want to hurt her.

Dropping his gaze from hers, he continued. "We fell into one of the bomb craters. Down through rubble. A piece of metal went all the way through my right leg."

Kensie gasped as he finished. "Rebel landed mostly on top of me, so the metal that went through me also sliced her back leg open pretty badly. I passed out. I woke up later in a helicopter airlifting me and Rebel out of there. Apparently the insurgents had come down from the other side and finished off the rest of my team."

"I'm so sorry," Kensie whispered, her hand like a vise on his shoulder.

"I guess they thought we were already dead. I was out cold, but Rebel wasn't. She must have kept totally still while they were searching. The team who came to help us said they wouldn't have even known we were down there except Rebel alerted them. We were flying out of the site and I was trying to stay conscious long enough to ask about my team, but no one wanted to answer me."

When they'd avoided the question, he'd known it was bad. But as hard as he'd tried, he hadn't been able to hold onto consciousness long enough to force the issue. It had been days later, in the hospital, when a representative from the military he'd never met before had finally broken the news.

"I had two surgeries, the first one to get the piece of metal out of me and then later to screw the leg back together to try and save it. Rebel had three, poor girl, though her leg has healed better than mine. Then there was PT for both of us, for a good six months. We both made it back home, but our career together was over."

His physical therapy had been driven by an equal mix of unrealistic determination to get himself back into fighting shape and the desire to just be mobile enough to go and see his brothers' families in person. Apologize.

He'd never done it. By the time he'd healed enough to be released, he'd broken down every time he'd picked up the phone to book the travel. Since then, one of his brothers' wives had given birth to their first child. Another's oldest had graduated from high school. So much they should have been around to see.

Instead, it had just been Colter. And no one had been waiting for him because he'd never made that commitment to anyone or anything outside the service.

It wasn't fair. But staring at Kensie now, as she sniffled and swiped a hand over her face, where tears ran freely, he realized how much had changed for him. For the first time since that day, he was actually glad he'd lived through it.

For this moment. Her hand clutching him so tightly as she tried to get control over her emotions. It wasn't pity in her eyes, but deep sadness and understanding.

He knew she understood why he'd never felt like he should have gotten another chance when none of his brothers had. Because somewhere deep down, she probably felt the same way about her sister.

But the bond he felt with her was more than one of loss. Because she made him want to live again, to reach for things he had no business wanting.

He couldn't do it.

She had a shot at finding Alanna, at moving on with her life and finding happiness. But how could he smile and go on with life like everything was fine when eight other families had buried their happiness?

The answer was simple. His living that day had been a fluke, an act of love from his partner. But it wasn't what was supposed to have happened. He should have gone with his brothers. And he wasn't going to betray them by leaving them behind a second time.

Chapter Fourteen

His leg was killing him.

Colter bit the inside of his lip until he tasted blood. He leaned heavily on the cane he'd reluctantly pulled out this morning when he'd discovered even getting out of his recliner was a challenge. He hadn't used the thing in more than six months, when he'd vowed never to rely on it again. Thank goodness he'd stashed it in a closet instead of tossing it.

He hated that he needed it now, but it was better than not being able to keep up with Kensie. Because as much as he could have used another day or two to recover, he knew she wasn't going to wait. And he didn't trust anyone else to help her.

She'd slept twenty feet away from him last night, tucked into his bed. Every time she'd rolled over, he'd heard the rustle of his sheets and every nerve in his body had fired to life. Especially since, before she'd headed to his room to sleep, she'd leaned over and pressed the softest, briefest kiss on his lips.

The feel of that kiss had lingered through the night, tingling every time he heard her move. Even before his accident, he'd never connected with anyone the way he had with Kensie.

He still couldn't believe he'd shared his story with her. Even more, he couldn't believe he'd done it without having a bad flashback or a panic attack. But her touch on his shoulder and Rebel's head under his hand had kept him grounded in the present.

Today, he felt wrung out from the inside. But in a strange way, it felt good, like some of the tension and anger he'd been carrying around for the past year had been swept away, too.

Maybe it was looking at the way she lived her life. She'd said she spent too long trying to do everything at two hundred percent to make up for what happened to her sister. But when he looked at Kensie, he didn't see a woman doing everything at warp speed to avoid having to really live. He saw someone capable and strong, someone who would never give up on the people she loved.

Right now she was walking beside him. He could practically feel her restrained energy as she took short strides, her hand resting on Rebel's head.

They'd agreed last night that, since her truck was in town and he was in no shape to drive, she'd stay with him. Then, today, they'd go back to the part of town where she'd spotted Henry. With all the stores open, they'd be able to talk to more people and hopefully get some better answers about the man and where he lived.

The plan had been to set off in the morning, but his leg had refused to hold his weight for very long. The concern on Kensie's face had mixed with an anxiousness to get going and he'd promised he'd be ready by midafternoon. She'd seemed doubtful, but here they were. He would be paying for this later, but he wasn't taking any chances. His pistol was holstered under his shirt on the left.

Danny Weston was still in a holding cell, so he wasn't an immediate concern. But Colter didn't know enough about Henry to have any clue what to expect if they found him. If Kensie was right and he'd had her sister for the past fourteen years, Colter wasn't messing around. Whatever it took to free Alanna, he was willing to do.

"How can no one know this guy?" Kensie asked now, sounding as frustrated as she looked.

They'd spoken to half the store owners so far, plus a handful of locals braving the cold. The temperatures weren't abnormal for this time of year—hovering around twenty degrees—but the windchill had been brutal all afternoon. He'd tugged up the collar of Kensie's coat for her, but her cheeks were already windburned.

"Someone will know," Colter promised.

It was clear Henry was trying to stay off people's radar, and while locals embraced the idea of "live and let live," they were also a wary bunch. You had to be, with people like Danny Weston trying to take advantage of that attitude.

So the locals might try to stay out of other people's business, but a guy like Henry would have raised flags for someone. They just had to find the right person—the one who'd not only gotten suspicious but was also in a position to notice details about where he might be hiding out.

And Colter had an idea who that right person might be. He held open the door to a check-cashing place that looked like it had been built fifty years ago and never cleaned in all that time. It was crammed into a corner of the town, mostly hidden behind a grocery/hardware store, but that's how the locals liked it—out of sight. And so did the people who frequented it. People who wanted as short a paper trail as possible, who didn't believe in keeping their money in banks.

"Let's try here," he suggested.

Kensie gave him a doubtful look but preceded him into the store, Rebel on her heels.

"That dog better be a service dog," the owner snapped. He was perpetually scowling, a guy who looked as unkempt and old as his store. But his eyes were sharp, zooming in on Colter's side immediately as if he could tell Colter was carrying.

"One of the best," Colter replied, purposely misunderstanding what the guy meant by "service."

The owner—Yura something—screwed his lips

up in a semiscowl, but his gaze drifted from Colter's side to his cane and his dragging leg. "Yeah, okay. You looking to cash a check?"

"No, I'm looking for some information on someone who might have been in here."

"Don't give out information on my customers," Yura said, turning his attention to the TV mounted in the corner, playing a soap opera on mute.

"We think he kidnapped my friend's sister," Colter said, nodding toward Kensie.

Yura narrowed his gaze on Kensie, then frowned harder at Colter. "What's his name?"

"Henry Rollings."

"Henry, huh?"

"You know him?" Kensie's voice was full of hope as she leaned closer to Yura.

"Yeah," Yura said slowly.

"What can you tell us about him?"

Yura stared so long at Colter that Colter thought he was going to have to ask again. Finally, Yura asked, "Why do you think he kidnapped this woman?"

"I saw her," Kensie blurted. "I tried to follow them and then someone else got in my way and Henry drove off with her."

Yura's gaze shifted briefly to Kensie, then returned to Colter. "You were a Marine, huh?"

Colter wasn't sure how Yura knew that, but he

supposed it was a sign his instincts were correct—
Yura noticed things about people. "That's right."

He nodded at Rebel. "Her, too?"

"Yes."

"So was I. Long time ago." Yura sighed heavily. "Henry's a strange guy. Lot of the people who come in here are hiding from something. Not really my business what it is. But kidnapping a woman? You sure about that?"

"No," Colter answered, sensing Yura would respond better to honesty. "But there's a really good chance. And if he did take her, he knows that we know. So we don't have long to find him."

"Please," Kensie said, her voice barely above a whisper. "If you can help us…"

Yura nodded. "Henry cashes checks in here sometimes. I think usually he gets paid in cash, but every once in a while he does odd jobs for a couple up north. Untrusting sort, the Altiers. They like to stay off the radar, too. They pay well but keep a couple of guns on hand and only pay by check. Say it's a safety thing and I don't blame them, the way they hire drifters. Plus, they've got a bunch of kids to think about."

"Up north?" Colter asked. "Is that where Henry lives? Near this couple?"

Yura dug around under the counter and then dropped a piece of torn notebook paper on it. He sketched out a rough map, then turned it around for Colter to see. "You know where this is?"

Colter held in a curse. "Yeah, I think so."

"I can't be sure he lives up that way, but if I had to guess, this is what I'd pick. The couple he works for is here." Yura tapped the hand-drawn map, marking a spot in the middle of nowhere. "No one lives within two miles of them. They're seriously paranoid. But Henry's come in here a half dozen times over the past few years with checks from them. My bet is he lives somewhere in this area, close enough that they feel comfortable hiring him repeatedly."

"It's out of the way," Colter agreed. "Perfect for someone who wants to hide. And in the direction that the warehouse owner said he sometimes sees Henry go."

"It's not going to be an easy area to get into unnoticed." Yura pushed the map toward him. "Semper Fi, brother."

Hearing the words sent a jolt through Colter, part shock, part energizing. It had been a year since anyone had spoken them to him. "Semper Fi."

"Thank you," Kensie added as she trailed Colter out the door. "How long will it take us to get there?"

"We're not going tonight."

"What?" She slapped her hands on her hips, over the warm coat he'd forced her to buy the other day. "Why not?"

Even though he knew it was windburn, he liked

the pink in her cheeks. It matched the fire in her eyes right now. But he wouldn't let himself be swayed. He'd agreed to help her find her sister, not get her killed in the process.

"For one, it's going to be dark in a couple of hours and we don't even know if he lives here. This is Yura's guess. Two, the terrain is seriously treacherous. We don't want to be stuck out there at night."

"Colter—"

"I know time is crucial, Kensie. Believe me, I get it. But we're not doing your sister any good if we get ourselves killed. And I'm not kidding about the area. There's no easy way to access it other than one trail, and even that's blocked half the time. We've already had enough of a snowfall that it's possible snow has dumped off the side of the hills and made it inaccessible."

"But we saw Henry in town just yesterday. He got here somehow."

"Yeah, and that probably tells us the road is fine, but some of the locals who live way out in the wilderness use snow mobiles and keep a vehicle somewhere else. Besides, if Henry is anticipating us, he'll know to watch that road. Not to mention that Yura's map just gives us a general area. It'll take us hours to investigate it all."

"So, maybe night is better," Kensie argued. "If Henry is watching the road—"

"We get people stuck up in that area who freeze

to death every year, Kensie. There are no cell towers for miles, so no cell service at all. And the houses are miles apart, too, so you'd be lucky to reach help."

"But you know the area—"

"Not that area. Not well enough. I'm not taking you up there tonight."

Frustration and disappointment mingled on her face, but they couldn't hide what was underneath: fear. Fear that even as they stood there speaking, Henry was already rushing her sister out of town. That they were already too late.

"Tomorrow morning," Colter promised. "We'll go with supplies and a plan. Okay?"

"Okay," she agreed reluctantly.

He nodded. "I'll drop you at your hotel so you can get fresh clothes and I'll pick you up tomorrow at eight. Sound good?"

"Oh. Sure."

The surprise in her voice told him she'd half-expected to go back to his cabin with him tonight. The idea made desire curl in his belly, but he ignored it.

He couldn't take her with him tonight because he wasn't going home.

After he dropped her off, he planned to scout the area himself.

SHE SHOULD BE with Colter now, not tossing and turning in her ridiculously soft hotel bed, unable to sleep. It was mostly worry about Alanna keeping her up, but part of it was the man helping her find her sister.

If they did locate Alanna tomorrow, Kensie would be going home. She'd never see Colter again. Just the thought of it made her chest tighten with dread.

Why hadn't she spoken up when he'd told her he'd drop her off at her hotel? Based on the way he'd returned her kiss last night before she'd headed off to his room, if she'd asked to go with him, he would have said yes. Instead of sitting here, heart beating too fast and a million different scenarios about what could happen tomorrow running through her mind, she could be with Colter right now.

In his bed with him. Or on his lap on his recliner. She'd even take a spot curled up on the floor by Rebel if it meant she could be close to Colter.

Who was she kidding? Even if she started out on the floor—which she knew Colter would never let happen—she wouldn't stay there long. She'd end up beside him, underneath him, on top of him, arms and legs entwined, lips pressed against his until she could hardly breathe.

Normally, she backed away from relationships that had too much potential to hurt her heart. Her mom said it was her way of protecting herself from losing anyone again. So she left them first.

It was probably true, but then, she'd never met anyone she couldn't stay away from. Until Colter.

His loss had been different than hers, but he understood the mingling of grief and guilt in a way most people couldn't. And maybe that was part of why she felt connected to him. But it was only a small part.

The rest of it was about the man. The way he'd risked his own safety for hers and Rebel's. The way he smiled at Rebel when she sat by him. The way he looked at her sometimes with those soft blue eyes, focused so intently on her as if he never wanted her to leave his side.

She knew exactly where it would lead to sleep with someone she cared too much about and then walk away. She'd never been remotely tempted to try it. But right now, she was pretty sure *not* staying with Colter tonight was going to be one of the biggest regrets of her life.

So do something about it. The thought hit like a sledgehammer and Kensie shoved off her covers, heart pounding. What would Colter do if she just showed up at his cabin tonight?

Only one way to find out. Kensie felt a goofy smile lifting her lips as she flipped on the light next to her bed.

As the light went on, there was a soft thump from the other side of her door.

Kensie froze, listening. Had Colter gotten the same idea and come to her hotel tonight? No. He'd never stand out there skulking if he'd made up his mind to be with her. He'd knock forcefully and then wait patiently for her to decide.

Maybe someone else had checked into the hotel. Except the sound had come from *right* outside her door. Too close to be someone going into another room.

Maybe she was imagining things. She sat perfectly still, straining to listen. Another sound reached her ears, this time a drawn-out metallic scrape, as if someone was working the lock.

She jerked in response, banging her head against the headboard as panic took hold.

At the sound, whoever was outside stopped being quiet. There was a loud *thud*, like a big body ramming against the door. The door actually curved inward near the ceiling, but the lock held.

Why had she chosen the big, luxurious failing hotel with hardly anyone staying in it instead of the beat-up motel closer to downtown? The only other person staying on this floor had checked out yesterday. The manager was four floors below her, probably asleep at his desk like he had been last night. Screaming was useless.

Fighting back panic, Kensie practically fell out of bed, groping for her cell phone. *Colter.* His number popped up first, the last person she'd texted.

Need help right now, she typed frantically, even as she wondered if she should call 911. But Colter knew exactly where she was, knew who was a threat to her in this town. Had Danny Weston been let out of jail already? Why wouldn't the police give her a heads-up?

She'd call the police as soon as she finished texting Colter. *Please hur—*

There was another thunderous *bang,* and this time the door burst inward, splintering away all around the lock.

Even knowing it was useless, Kensie screamed. Dropping the phone, she grappled blindly for anything she could use as a weapon, her gaze locked on the man backlit in her doorway.

Not Danny. Henry Rollings.

He rushed into the room, igniting a million fragments of memory in her mind. Alanna glancing back and smiling at her as she danced. The tire swing her dad had hung in the front yard. A big dark sedan rolling slowly down the street toward them. A quick hand reaching out and yanking Alanna away.

Everything suddenly sped up, in her memory and right in front of her, as Henry darted around the foot of the bed.

He was older than he'd been fourteen years ago, more gray in his hair, more lines on his face. But he still outweighed her by a lot, still had ropey muscle in his forearms and a dangerous gleam in his eyes.

"You never should have come here," he said, his voice low and deadly.

Kensie stopped groping for a weapon. Instead, she leaped on top of the bed. Running instead of fighting suddenly seemed like her best option.

He changed direction, reaching for her, but she jumped over his arm, landing awkwardly on the floor on the other side of the bed.

Something pierced her bare foot and pain exploded in her arch, but Kensie ignored it, her focus solely on the door. She could hear him behind her, catching up, and she ran faster, tears pricking her eyes at what she realized was a splinter from the broken door in her foot.

She was so close. If she could just get through the door, the emergency exit for the stairs was a straight shot down the hallway. There was a fire alarm right next to it she could pull on her way, maybe attracting attention from the hotel staff who knew she was up here.

She'd almost cleared the door when a big hand closed like a vise around her elbow and yanked her back into the room, hard enough to send her to the ground. Her head smacked the floor and even the thick carpeting wasn't enough of a cushion to stop the shock. The air whooshed out of her lungs and her vision wavered briefly.

Then he was kneeling over her, one knee on either side of her hips, and a new kind of panic exploded in her chest. What was he going to do to her? What had he done to her sister?

Tears filled her eyes, but rage almost instantly overtook the fear as she thought of Alanna. Where was her sister right now? Was Henry planning to get rid of Kensie so he could continue hiding here with her sister?

But it was too late for that. Colter knew about him. Even if she was gone, Colter would search for Alanna.

It wouldn't come to that, Kensie vowed. Yanking her arms upward before he could pin them down, Kensie used her nails and went straight for his eyes.

He jerked out of the way just in time, but before she could use his shifted position to her advantage, he was back, leaning closer. Blowing rancid breath in her face, he snarled, "I don't know how you found me, but you're not taking me down."

With his face so close to hers, Kensie instinctively tried to shift her head away. Then she realized her mistake and went after him again, this time getting her nails deep in the skin of his cheek as he jerked backward.

But it wasn't enough. Calling her all kinds of names, Henry pressed his big hands around her neck. They closed around it with ease and then he was pushing down, stealing all her air.

"I didn't even know she had a sister," Henry growled. "You should have let her go. Let *me* go."

Kensie gagged, grabbing his hands with hers, trying to peel them off. But he was even stronger than he looked. Spots formed in front of her eyes, even as she kicked up, trying to knee him in the groin.

He moved his knees inward, pressing her legs together, keeping them pinned to the ground. His hands closed tighter around her neck, his lips moving into a satisfied smile before his face started to blur.

Kensie flailed, a last desperate attempt to break his chokehold, but it was no use. She couldn't breathe; she could barely see.

She was going to die.

She would never know what happened to her sister. She was going to put her family through the trauma of losing another member. She was going to put Colter through the grief of losing someone else who mattered to him. Because, as gruff as he acted, she knew he cared for her.

He'd never know how much she cared about him.

Kensie's hands shook as she tried to peel Henry's fingers away from her neck, tried to gasp in another breath. But none came.

Her hands stopped working. She felt them hit the carpet beside her, useless, as everything went dark.

Chapter Fifteen

Kensie wasn't answering. Not her cell phone and not the phone in her room.

Warning Rebel, "Hang on, girl," Colter jammed his foot down on the gas.

Rebel lurched forward anyway, letting out a brief whine.

"Sorry, girl," he said, both hands clenched tightly on the wheel as he took the unpaved road way too fast. His truck bounced and rattled, sliding on sudden patches of ice, but always gaining traction again.

Why wasn't Kensie answering? Her text had cut off midsentence and that had been several minutes ago, with nothing since.

Colter gritted his teeth as he took another curve at speeds that made his truck teeter right. It set back down again, earning another warning whine from Rebel. But he was all the way out by where Henry Rollings might live, using the map Yura had given them earlier. Despite the dangerous roads, he needed speed to get to Kensie.

"Call 911," he told his phone, glancing down to be sure it picked up his voice properly. If the police thought he was overreacting, so be it.

"Nine-one-one. What's your emergency?"

"This is Colter Hayes." He didn't know the voice on the other end of the line, but it was a small town, so hopefully whoever it was recognized his name and knew he wasn't prone to false alarms or overreactions. "My…" he stumbled over "friend," the word not feeling right on his tongue, then he hurried on "…is in trouble. She just texted me that she needed help. She's staying at that big luxury hotel outside of town."

"I need you to stay calm, sir," the woman replied, her own voice way too even and slow, making him realize he'd been talking at warp speed. "What kind of trouble is she in?"

"I don't know. She didn't give me any details. Her text cut off midsentence and she's not picking up her phone. I need police to get there now."

"Okay, sir, we'll send someone out to see what's happening," she said in that same exasperatingly slow voice, telling him she definitely didn't know who he was. "But do you think it's possible she just needed help with something simple? That it's not an emergency?"

"No, I don't think that's possible! She'd never text me to hurry if it weren't an emergency." His voice gained volume with every word and he took a deep breath, trying to stay calm. "Are officers on their way?"

As he asked, he left the treacherous unpaved trail he hadn't wanted Kensie on tonight for a smoother road. At the transition, his truck bounced high enough that his head almost smacked the cab ceiling. In the rearview, he saw Rebel hunkered down, trying not to get thrown around.

At least Kensie was staying at the overpriced luxury hotel outside of Desparre instead of the cheap motel downtown. He was much closer to the hotel. Of course, the police were closer to town. But then, it was late enough that probably no one was left at the station anyway.

"Who lives out by the luxury hotel? I want the closest officer sent out."

"Don't worry, sir. We'll get someone over there to check it out. Now, I want you to remain calm and—"

"She's on the fourth floor, room 409." He cut her off, then hung up. He didn't want to waste time with her focused on his panic. Not when he needed every bit of his attention on the dangerous roads ahead.

"It's going to be okay, girl," he told Rebel, partly because he knew he was making the ride hard for her and partly to reassure himself about Kensie.

She had to be okay. He didn't think he could handle losing someone else.

The very thought of something happening to

Kensie made his breath stutter and his lungs lock up as his heartbeat thundered painfully against his chest.

Not this. Not now.

A hundred curses screamed in his mind, but he couldn't get enough air to voice them. He clenched the wheel harder and eased his foot up off the gas, fighting the panic and impending dizziness. He couldn't afford to lose control, especially not here, not at speeds his truck could barely handle with him on full alert.

Suddenly, Rebel's nose pressed against his arm and he realized she'd stood and pushed her head between the seats. He breathed deeply, slowly, focusing on the feel of her head leaning into his biceps.

"Thanks, girl," he said when the panic eased and his heart rate started to slow.

He could do this. He wasn't going to let his mind wander to all the possible reasons Kensie had sent that text, all the possible dangers she could be facing. He was going to put all of his energy into getting to her as fast as he could.

"I've got this, girl," he told Rebel, pleased when his voice came out strong and determined. "Lay back down," he told her, not wanting her to get thrown around as he punched the gas again.

She listened, obviously sensing he'd conquered his panic.

"Call Kensie," he ordered his phone, but once

again, it went to voice mail. Instead of hanging up immediately, he said, "Hang on, Kensie. I'm coming."

Then he jammed the gas pedal into the floorboards. The turns came too fast as he put the truck's suspension to a serious test. It still seemed to take forever to get to the hotel, but he knew it was less than ten minutes since Kensie had texted.

Squealing to a stop, Colter yanked the truck into Park and then grabbed his cane before jumping out of the cab. Rebel was right behind him, so fast that he suspected she knew Kensie needed them.

But where were the police cruisers, sirens wailing? Instead, the parking lot was dark and silent, only a few vehicles scattered up near the entrance.

Colter swore as he pushed his leg as hard as he could, doing a ridiculous hobble-run to the front of the hotel, not even bothering to shut the truck door behind him. Rebel kept pace beside him, tension in the lines of her back that told him she was ready for battle.

When they burst through the doors into the hotel lobby, the older man behind the desk jerked his head up in surprise. "Can I help—"

"Have you seen Kensie Morgan? She's staying—"

"Fourth floor," the man interrupted. "From Chicago. Nice lady. She—"

"Have you seen her in the past ten minutes?" Colter demanded.

"No."

"She's in trouble. Call the police." Colter didn't care that he'd already done it. The fact that they weren't here yet—regardless of how far the drive was for the closest officer—pissed him off.

"What?" The man pressed a shaky hand to his chest. "What's going on?"

Colter didn't answer. He just bolted for the elevator and jammed his hand against the Up button. If he'd been in fighting shape, stairs would be quicker, even at four stories. But these days, elevators were a faster option.

Thankfully, the elevator must have been at the ground floor, because it opened up fast and then he and Rebel were inside it, heading up. "Please be okay," he chanted, watching the numbers beep by as they rose too slowly.

Finally the elevator arrived with a loud *ding* and Colter slid through before the doors finished opening. Rebel charged out after him.

He'd never been up here, but over the blood racing in his ears, he heard…something. Almost like a gurgling. And way down the hall, something lying in the hallway. Small, like a piece of wood. But it didn't belong.

Colter headed that way, almost stumbling as he pushed his leg as hard as he could. Rebel ran beside him, following his silent command.

Before he reached the room, the noise stopped. When he finally peered inside, Henry Rollings glanced back from where he knelt on the floor.

And beneath him was Kensie, her head lolled to one side and her eyes closed.

WITH A ROAR that didn't even sound like him, Colter dropped his cane and rushed Rollings.

Panic shot across Henry's face as he tried to scramble to his feet. But he wasn't fast enough.

Leaning on his stronger left leg, Colter grabbed the man by a fistful of shirt and yanked him off Kensie and onto his back. Not letting him regroup, Colter let go of his shirt and grabbed him by the forearm, twisting up and back as he dragged Henry farther away from Kensie.

"Check Kensie, girl," he told Rebel, who leaped right over Henry and landed beside Kensie.

Colter said a silent prayer that she was okay, but right now he had to focus on neutralizing Henry before the guy realized Colter's weakness and went for his bad leg like Danny had.

From the corner of his eye, Colter watched as Rebel nudged Kensie, then did it again, harder. Kensie didn't move and Colter felt panic rising inside of him.

Then Henry yelped and twisted, yanking his arm free while Colter was distracted. Pushing against the floor for leverage, Henry shoved himself upward.

Colter's panic shifted into rage. His focus narrowed onto just Henry, all of his fury and fear directed at the man. He could feel his lips twisting back into a snarl as he raised his fist.

He'd been to war, survived multiple tours where he'd seen others die. He'd faced an enemy with the desire to eliminate a threat, but he'd never felt this kind of primal hatred before. His fist connected with Henry's face, fueled by all of that rage, too hard and fast for the man to block it.

Henry hit the ground hard, lights out.

For a split second, Colter wanted to keep pounding on him. But his worry for Kensie quickly overcame his hatred for Henry.

Colter twisted toward her. His knee popped as he dropped down beside her. His eyes watered at the pain, but he brushed the moisture away and pressed his fingers to her bruised neck. Rebel let out a long, low whine as Colter prayed.

Then he felt it. A pulse. Slow, too weak, but it was there.

Dropping even lower, he placed his hand in front of her mouth and nose, waiting for the soft brush of her breath. It, too, was faint but there.

Suddenly, he couldn't see as he stroked his hand down her cheek. "Kensie, Kensie, wake up." A drop splattered on her face and he realized he was crying.

Her eyes blinked open, confusion and pain in her gaze. "Wha—" she croaked.

"Don't try to talk." He sucked in a long breath of relief, swiped away tears so he could see her better, then folded her hand in his. It felt so fragile, so delicate. "You're okay. You're okay."

Beside him, Rebel's tail thumped the ground and she dropped to her belly, resting her head on Kensie's arm.

Down the hall, he heard the *ding* of the elevator and footsteps running toward them. "We're in here," he called. "We need an ambulance."

"Colter Hayes?" a voice called back.

Chief Hernandez had come herself. It had taken way longer than Colter would have liked, but he knew the chief didn't live nearby. If she was the closest, then she'd still made good time.

"Yes. We're in here. Kensie needs an ambulance."

Kensie started to lift her head, but Colter put a hand on her shoulder. "Don't move."

He glanced back as Chief Hernandez poked her head around the door, then entered, holstering her weapon and lifting her radio. "Get me an ambulance."

She strode into the room and cuffed Henry's hands behind his back as he groaned and started moving.

"Where's Alanna?" Kensie croaked, her words barely intelligible.

It hurt Colter just to hear her speak. Neither his hand on her shoulder nor the chief's admonishment not to move until an EMT had looked at her prevented her from struggling to a sitting position.

Colter braced his hand behind her back and Rebel jumped up, rotating her body until she was sitting half behind Kensie for support.

"Good girl," he told Rebel, but she didn't even wag her tail in acknowledgment, just kept her serious gaze on Kensie.

"Where is she?" Kensie demanded, her voice raw but gaining volume.

Chief Hernandez yanked Henry to his feet and he groaned some more, shaking his head.

Trusting Rebel to have Kensie's back—literally—Colter stood, ignoring the new stiffness in his knee. He got in Henry's face even as the chief gave him a warning look and angled the hip where her weapon was holstered away from him.

"Where's Alanna Morgan?" he demanded, so close he could feel Henry's disgusting breath on his neck. "If I have to repeat my question, it won't matter that there's a cop here."

"Colter..." Chief Hernandez's voice was full of warning, but also worry.

She'd known him since he moved here. He'd even helped her break up a bar fight once when her backup was slow and his leg was in a cooperative mood. For the most part, they got along. But she'd never heard this tone from him. And he knew if he had to make good on his threat, she'd have to do her duty and protect the guy in cuffs.

But he wasn't going to let Henry hide behind an arrest now. "Tell me," he growled.

Henry's face went pale as his gaze darted to Kensie. "I don't know what you're talking about."

"Colter," the chief snapped before he could respond. She yanked Henry back a few steps and he went willingly with her. Then her backup was in the room, a couple of cops Colter probably could have taken down in better days, but not now.

"Colter." Kensie's softer voice came from behind him.

He turned and realized she'd gotten to her feet. She sounded and looked terrible, with blue and purple streaks all the way across the front of her throat. But her balance was steady and her eyes were clear.

"Let me do this," she croaked.

"Everyone just calm down," the chief said as the other officers stood in front of Kensie, blocking Henry. "Jennings, give me your fingerprint kit."

"Hey, *he* attacked *me*," Henry shouted, starting to struggle.

"And you broke into this hotel room and attacked the occupant," the chief replied calmly as she yanked her arm upward, pulling his cuffed hands up, too.

Henry yelped and then Jennings was pressing his finger into a machine the size of a cell phone as the other officer kept his gaze locked on Colter and his hand locked over his pistol.

"This is pretty cool, huh?" Jennings asked, excitement in his flushed cheeks and too-high tone. "Pretty much only the FBI has these, but we got a grant after this serial case a few years ago and…oh."

"What?" the chief asked as Jennings stared at the machine.

He turned it toward her and she shook her head. "Guess we know why you didn't want us to take your prints, now, don't we, Manny Henderson?"

Henry/Manny let out a string of curses, then insisted, "I didn't kill her."

At his words, Kensie whimpered and Colter spun, grabbing her as she swayed.

But she pushed him off, tears streaming down her cheeks as she rushed forward. She leaned around the officer who stood in her way, croaking, "You killed my sister?"

"Look, I didn't even know Shoshana had a sister," Henry said. "But I didn't kill her. Someone framed me, okay? I ran because someone framed me."

"What?" Kensie and Colter asked together.

Chief Hernandez sighed loudly. "Manny Henderson here skipped town in Kansas a decade ago after murdering Shoshana Lewis."

"I didn't kill her!" Manny shouted.

Ignoring him, the chief continued, "Apparently he's been hiding out here ever since."

Kensie dropped to the floor so fast Colter didn't have time to move. He realized belatedly that it was a semicontrolled fall as she sat and buried her head in her hands.

"He didn't come after me because of Alanna," she whispered.

"Who the heck is Alanna?" Henry snapped.

From the floor, Kensie looked up at Colter and he knelt closer, ignoring the way his knee protested. "He thought I knew about the murder in Kansas. When I said I was from the Midwest…" A sob burst out, then she turned her gaze on Henry. "I was wrong. He looked so much like the guy I remember, but he had nothing to do with Alanna's kidnapping."

"I didn't kidnap anyone!" Henry yelled. "And I didn't kill anyone, either. I was—"

"Get him out of here," Chief Hernandez demanded, pushing Henry toward Jennings, then stepping closer to Kensie.

"I'm so sorry," she told Kensie. "But I think you're right. You stumbled onto a fugitive. And I know I could have been more patient with you before, but the FBI really did work hard when they came up here. I don't think the note was real."

"I've been chasing a ghost," Kensie whispered, staring into the space where Henry had been.

"I think it's time you go home," the chief said.

A jolt of dismay shot through Colter as Kensie's defeated voice agreed. "I think you're right."

Chapter Sixteen

It was time to go home.

The very idea made Kensie want to curl up in a ball and weep. But she just gritted her teeth harder, until her jaw and her head hurt.

"Are you in pain?"

Blinking moisture away, Kensie looked up at the nurse checking her vitals. "No," she croaked, even though speaking made her throat feel like she'd shoved sandpaper down there and was scrubbing as hard as possible. Then again, not speaking didn't feel much better.

Apparently, her throat was so swollen the doctors had considered putting a tube in to help her breathe. But she'd fought them on it until they'd agreed to keep her under observation and on some kind of intravenous medicine for a while.

For the past few hours, she'd been here alone. Colter and Rebel had come with her in the ambulance, but they wouldn't let the dog in the hospital no matter how much Colter argued. So finally he'd agreed to go to the police station and give his statement while doctors checked her out.

"You're doing good, hon," the nurse said, patting her arm and leaving the room.

Once she was gone, Kensie stared blankly into the empty room, still feeling blindsided. Henry Rollings's claims that he hadn't killed the woman in Kansas had been forced and full of denial. His confusion about her sister had sounded so real.

Even though he was a killer, Kensie believed him when he said he didn't know Alanna. He'd come after her because he thought she was onto his real identity and the murder he'd committed in Kansas. She'd played right into his fears when she'd told him she was from the Midwest instead of being specific and saying Chicago.

So whoever she'd seen that day with Henry wasn't Alanna. It couldn't have been. It was another woman, someone who just resembled what Alanna might have looked like if she'd had the chance to grow up.

Because the truth was, Alanna had probably never gotten that chance.

Kensie knew the statistics about stranger child abductions. Her family had come to accept the truth long ago. And Kensie had been running from it ever since her parents had given in and decided to move on with their lives.

Instead of following their example, she'd chased a ghost, seeing leads where there were none because she was so desperate to undo a mistake she'd made when she was thirteen. Maybe it was time to forgive herself. Maybe it was time to let Alanna go.

The sob that burst forward made Kensie choke and gag. Her throat felt like it was closing up and her chest felt like it was on fire. A nurse ran into the room as Kensie got control of her breathing. She swiped the tears off her face and managed, "I'm okay."

She wasn't. But hopefully she would be.

Her parents' wake-up call had been Flynn's accident. Apparently she'd needed a fugitive to try and kill her to find her own wake-up call.

"Kensie?" Colter's voice reached her from the hallway.

She stared at the open doorway and then he appeared, moving as fast as he could with his cane. Kensie closed her eyes and held out her arms.

Then his arms were around her and her head was on his chest. She squeezed her eyes more tightly closed, breathing in Colter's scent—clean and slightly musky—and tried to relax. Because as badly as she needed a good cry, doing it would hurt too much. And she didn't want a sedative or a tube in her throat.

Finally, he leaned back and stared down at her face, brushing hair out of her eyes. "Are you okay?"

She nodded, not wanting to speak, not even sure she *could* speak without losing it.

He didn't move his arms from around her and she kept hers looped around his back. It felt right, like something she'd do with a boyfriend instead of a man she'd only known for a few days.

"I gave the police my statement, Kensie, and the reason it took me so long to get back here—besides dropping Rebel off somewhere safe—is that I talked to them about Henry."

From the way his lips twisted up, she knew bad news was coming. She held on tighter, waiting.

"They've contacted police in Kansas and I asked the chief to beg for a little professional courtesy and get the station there to look into his whereabouts when your sister went missing."

Kensie's heart thumped madly, a brief hope, but he shook his head.

"The day Alanna disappeared, Henry Rollings was serving a one-month jail sentence for a DUI. He's not the guy, Kensie. I'm so sorry."

She ducked her head, pressing her face against his chest and letting the relief and disappointment roll over her in waves. Relief because Henry was a killer, but he hadn't killed Alanna. Disappointment because, yet again, she had no real answers.

And it was time to accept that maybe she never would.

She wasn't sure how long she stayed there, not moving, but she didn't want to let go. Her time in Alaska was about to end and that meant leaving Colter behind.

She was falling for him more with every day. There was no question about it. But that wasn't enough.

Not when he was too broken to move on with his life, even if he cared for her, too.

Besides, her family was waiting for her. A family who'd been scared for her to come here, who hadn't been whole for too long but had always tried. They'd stood by each other instead of letting Alanna's loss tear them apart. And even though she blamed herself, they'd never blamed her. Not once, even in anger, had anyone suggested it was her fault. Except for Kensie herself.

Leaving Desparre—leaving Colter—was the right thing to do. So why did it feel so wrong?

HE DIDN'T WANT to let her go.

Colter glanced at Kensie, sitting silently in the passenger seat of his truck, staring out the window. In the past four days, he'd come to think of it as her seat. And now she was leaving.

In the back, Rebel sat quietly beside Kensie's suitcase. His dog had let out a low whine when Colter loaded it and he'd petted her softly. "I know, girl," he'd whispered. "I know."

The doctors had cleared Kensie to leave this afternoon and she'd booked a flight home tonight. In the brief time between, they'd held hands and walked the streets of Desparre without speaking.

Then he'd left her at her hotel to pack while he picked up Rebel so they could both say goodbye.

He couldn't believe he was about to drop her off at the airport and never see her again.

Stealing a glance at her, he tried to memorize her profile. The thick, glossy hair framing her face. The full lips, always tilted slightly up at the corners like she was on the verge of a smile. She was staring out the window, so he couldn't see her eyes well, but he didn't need to. He could picture the exact shade of light brown, like a delicious toffee. He could see the serious intensity there.

Redirecting his attention to the road ahead, Colter blew out a heavy breath. He never used to be the guy who didn't know what to say, but since Kensie had told him she was leaving, he'd been at a complete loss for words.

He'd known it was coming eventually, of course. He even knew it was the right thing for her. But knowing it was different from watching her walk out of his life for good.

Don't go wanted so badly to erupt from his mouth, but he squeezed his lips closed. She had a family to return to, a life to rebuild—and maybe to rethink. In the hospital, he'd seen it on her face that she was reevaluating the choices she'd made in her life. He hoped she'd keep playing the violin. Even though he knew she'd chosen the career path because of Alanna, he could see it on her face when she talked about playing: she loved it.

He'd never get to see her play. Never meet her family or walk hand in hand with her down the street in comfortable silence again.

And for the first time in a long time, he knew exactly what he wanted: her. He could picture a life with her. A home. Babies.

It was an impossible dream. But it felt good to dream again. He actually felt *alive* in a way he hadn't since the moment that first shot had rung out in the desert and Rebel had slammed into him.

"Kensie—"

She turned toward him, her face full of expectation and hope.

Words about staying in touch, about making plans to see each other down the road—someday, somehow—died on his lips. She deserved more than empty promises.

What could he really offer her from 3,500 miles away? A relationship of phone calls? The burden on her to fly out to see him since he'd vowed to remain in Desparre, since the very idea of going anywhere else made his chest hurt?

She was falling for him. He'd felt it in the lingering touch of her fingers on his face as she kissed him the other night. He saw it in the way she stared at him now, with the kind of unrealistic hope she'd once shown for finding her sister.

He might not be worthy of her, but he cared enough about her to try and do what was best for her. And that was giving her a clean break. As much as it hurt, what she needed most from him now was for him to let her go.

He slowed his truck to a stop in front of the airport, unable to believe how fast the time had come. "I'm going to miss you, Kensie."

Her mouth opened into a silent O, the hope in her gaze fading. Then she gave him a forced, trembling smile. "Thank you for helping me, Colter."

She unbuckled her seat belt and twisted to pet Rebel, pressing her cheek briefly to his dog's head. "I'm going to miss you, Rebel."

Rebel whined, looking at Colter as if trying to tell him, "Make her stay, stupid."

Everything in him ached to comply, to beg Kensie not to go, or at least to stay in touch. Instead, he gave her his own forced smile. "We're going to miss you, Kensie."

She threw her arms around his neck, pressed a brief kiss to his lips and then stepped out of his truck. She grabbed her luggage from the back seat and strode into the airport before he could recover.

And then she was gone.

Chapter Seventeen

How could her heart feel this full and this empty at the same time?

Kensie stared out the window at the plane pulling up to her gate. It had only been four days ago that she'd left Chicago, terrified and full of hope for what she might find in Desparre. She'd never expected to find someone like Colter. She'd never expected to lose someone like Colter.

And she'd never thought she'd be returning home without Alanna and with a total loss of hope of ever finding her. The idea of giving up on her sister made guilt gnaw at her, but it was time to move on. Colter had taught her that. If only she could have taught him the same.

She didn't like picturing him and Rebel alone in their cabin, cloistered away from the world with only pictures of their dead brothers to sustain them. It wasn't a way to live. She wanted so much more for him.

But she couldn't force him to change. And she'd

spent too much of her life living for someone else. It was time she started living for herself.

As much as it hurt, she had to go. For the briefest moment, she'd thought he was going to suggest they stay in touch, maybe even pursue something long-distance. If he had, if he'd felt as strongly as she did, she would have ignored her head telling her it would never work. She would have followed her heart.

But he'd simply said goodbye, so she'd tried to do the same. A clean break. It was the right thing for both of them.

She'd practically run from his truck when he stopped outside the airport. If she'd dawdled, she knew she would have broken down, or worse yet, admitted how she felt about him. And telling a guy you were falling in love with him after knowing him for four days wasn't the best idea. Especially when you were about to leave and never talk to him again.

That wasn't how she wanted him to remember her, as needy and heartsick. She wanted him to remember her as strong and determined. She wanted him to think of her and recall the feel of her kiss, the warmth of her smile. Not an awkward goodbye.

"Are you okay, honey?"

Kensie looked up at the elderly woman holding out a tissue to her. She took it, nodding her head and swiping at tears she hadn't even realized she was shedding.

The woman frowned but walked away, and Kensie stiffened her shoulders. It was time to stop looking backward. Even if he didn't know it, Colter had done so much for her. She'd always cherish him for that.

Being with him had made her look at herself differently. She'd seen herself through his eyes and it had made her want things she never even knew she was missing.

Colter had looked at her, not knowing the accomplished violinist, the steadfast volunteer for cold-case searches. He'd seen *her.* He'd looked at her and seen her determination and her optimism and even her stubborn side and he'd liked her for those things alone. Staring back at him, she'd realized she'd spent her whole life measuring herself by the wrong things. And suddenly, she wanted more for herself.

More than a life lived in the spaces between searching for a sister she hadn't seen since she was a child. It wasn't her fault Alanna was gone. The person who'd kidnapped Alanna was to blame. And maybe by not living her own life to the fullest, Kensie was doing her sister's memory a disservice.

Alanna had only been five when she'd disappeared, but Kensie wasn't putting a shiny fantasy on her memory. Alanna had loved Kensie for playing games with her, reading to her before sleep and for the silly humor they shared. Those were the memories Kensie needed to keep alive, not a single moment she couldn't change.

"Now boarding for Flight 1850 to Seattle with continuing service to Chicago. Boarding all rows, all seats."

The announcement startled her and Kensie glanced up, realizing the plane had already off-boarded and been cleaned while she sat thinking about Colter and her life. She watched a short line of people file up to the entrance.

It felt like a lifetime since she'd been in Chicago. Closing her eyes, Kensie whispered, "Goodbye, Alanna."

Saying the words out loud seemed to lift a weight off of her. Her breathing actually came easier, even with the lingering pain in her throat and chest.

Her trip had been a failure, but she would be forever grateful she'd come. Colter had opened up a new world for her. If only she could have done the same for him.

Standing, Kensie shouldered her travel purse and joined the last of the passengers. She'd just handed her ticket to the gate agent when a familiar voice startled her.

"Kensie! Wait!"

Her heart seemed to give an extra-hard thump as she spun toward Colter.

He was running toward her as fast as his cane would allow, and dread and hope mingled. A long-distance relationship with a man who still couldn't move past his own grief was the wrong decision when she was finally trying to move forward. And yet, if he asked, there was no way she'd refuse.

"Colter," she breathed, envisioning trips to Alaska, warm nights in his bed, love letters to hold them over between visits.

He slid to a stop and her heart took off, unable to believe he'd come back for her. Heck, he'd probably bought a ticket just to get in here. To ask her in person instead of over the phone.

"Yes," she agreed before he could say anything.

The challenges of long distance didn't matter. The fact that he wasn't in the right place in his own life to enter into a relationship didn't matter either. They'd make it work. If he cared about her a fraction as much as she'd started to care for him, they'd figure it out.

"Kensie," he said, "Don't go."

Her heart pounded even faster. She had to leave now. Her family was waiting. She had so many decisions about her life to make back home. But she could come back. Soon.

Before she could voice any of that, he rushed on, "I think we were wrong. There's still a chance your sister is here. I think we can find her."

SHE WAS GOING to stay.

Thank goodness he'd pushed his leg so hard and gotten to the gate in time. If he'd been a minute or two later, Kensie would have already been gone. And even though he'd convinced himself he could let her go, the relief he felt right now was overwhelming.

"Final boarding for Flight 1850 to Seattle, with continuing service to Chicago," boomed over the speakers. "Passenger Kensie Morgan, please proceed to Gate 17. Aircraft doors close in two minutes."

Kensie blinked at him, then glanced over her shoulder at the aircraft entrance.

Colter dropped his cane and gripped her upper arms, wanting to shake off the incomprehension on her face. "Kensie. Did you hear me? I think we were wrong. We still have a shot at finding Alanna."

She turned back to face him, creases forming between her eyebrows. Her lips turned up in what he'd come to recognize as her apologetic look. "Colter, I…"

"Kensie." This time, he actually did shake her a little. "I talked to Jasper," he said quickly as Kensie glanced again at the airplane, as if she was actually still considering leaving on it.

Colter talked even faster, wondering what had happened since he'd dropped her off. Yesterday, if he'd suggested the remote possibility of a lead, she would have jumped up immediately. She would have ignored all the dangers, optimistically insisting this time could be it.

Then again, someone had just tried to kill her. And while being in the military meant he'd gotten used to being a target, he'd never had violence get so up close and personal, either. People trying to shoot you in a war zone was one thing; breaking into your hotel in a quaint Alaskan town and trying to choke you to death was another.

Sliding his hands down her arms, he twined his fingers with hers, and she finally gave him some real eye contact. "I know there have been a lot of dead ends. And some scary threats, between Henry and Danny. But this is different. I can feel it."

He wasn't just saying it to get her to stay. Jasper had repeatedly said he couldn't be sure of anything. But underneath his words, there'd been a restrained excitement, as if even he thought he was onto something.

"Jasper said a guy just came through his store asking about all the hubbub with the FBI and wanting to know if they'd given up already." He squeezed her hands a little tighter. "Kensie, Jasper remembers this guy from the day the note was found. This guy could have been with the girl he saw, the one he thought looked like you. Jasper said seeing this guy brought it all back. He says that day he assumed it was the guy's daughter with him."

Kensie's gaze darted to the gate and then back to him as they called her name once more over the speaker. "Did he say what this guy looked like?"

"No. But we can go and talk to him. He's waiting for us right now. I told him I was coming to get you and we'd be over as fast as we could."

She stared down at their locked hands a long moment, then shook her head. "Colter, I can't spend my life chasing long shot leads." She raised her head and there was something new in her eyes, something strong and bright. "I deserve to find my own life, to figure out what I want for *me*. You taught me that," she added softly.

He had? Her words made him sway backward slightly. He wanted that for her, but… "There's a time to move on, Kensie. But right now is the time for blind hope and optimism."

She started to shake her head, to pull her hands free, and he held on tighter.

"*You* taught me that," he told her. "You don't give up on the people you love."

Saying the words made him flinch a little, thinking about the day his brothers had died. Thinking about whether he was inadvertently leading her in the wrong direction, trying to force her attention back into her past when she had a real shot at a good future. But his gut was screaming at him that this was a true lead, and he wasn't sure he could follow it on his own.

Her shoulders dropped and hurt passed across her face, but just as quickly, she lifted her chin. "How do you know this isn't another dead end?"

"I don't," he said as the attendant at the gate announced, "Doors are closing for Flight 1850."

His leg was starting to throb from putting weight on it for so long, but he ignored it and pulled her a little closer. "Kensie, please come with me. This isn't over."

She stared up into his face for a long moment, then pulled her hands free. "It's not over," she repeated softly.

Then, she launched herself into his arms.

Chapter Eighteen

Kensie sneaked another glance at Colter, heart pounding madly. She was in the passenger seat of his truck, flying away from the airport at speeds that couldn't be legal. All of his attention was on the road ahead, his knuckles white against the steering wheel like he was on a mission.

She still couldn't believe she'd walked away from her flight. There wasn't another one to Chicago for three days.

Three more days with Colter. He was a dangerous temptation she needed to resist. Because whether it was three days from now on the very next flight, or three days after that, she'd eventually be leaving. And when it came to Colter, nothing had changed.

Falling halfway in love with him already meant heartache was waiting for her. Falling right into his arms would only make it worse.

"I'm glad you're staying, Kensie," Colter said, shooting her a sideways glance, as if he could feel her eyes on him.

When she'd thrown her arms around him at the airport, he'd actually lifted her off her feet and pressed his lips to hers for a long, tantalizing moment. People around them had cheered, clearly misunderstanding what was happening.

Now that they were back in his truck, she could read his nerves in the tense lines of his arms, the flexing of his jaw. He was worried he'd talked her into staying for just one more false lead.

Fear and hope blended, making her heart race even faster and her fingers tap a nervous beat against the armrest until Rebel pushed her nose between the seats and stilled her hand.

Kensie smiled at the dog, realizing how much she was going to miss Rebel, too, once she actually did leave. The thought added anxiety to the mix and Kensie took a deep breath.

This is just like every other lead on Alanna, she reminded herself. *Approach it like you always try to, with low expectations but high hopes.* It was a hard balance, but one she'd gotten fairly good at over the years.

But this time felt different. Maybe because she'd finally decided to let Alanna go and then gotten yanked right back into the search. It really felt like her last chance.

"I'm sorry."

It took her a minute to comprehend Colter's words and then she frowned over at him. Had she spoken out loud?

"I should have followed this lead on my own, instead of dragging you back into it. I was being selfish. I'm sorry."

Selfish? He'd spent the past four days running down leads on someone law enforcement had already given up on. He'd rushed to her side whenever she needed him, twice saving her from dangerous men.

Kensie let out a snort of disbelief. "Nothing you've done since I've known you has been selfish."

He was silent for a long time as they navigated the long drive back toward Desparre. Finally, as the roads beneath them changed from pavement to dirt, he spoke slowly, deliberately. "I didn't want you to go."

His words stunned her briefly into silence, but while her mouth refused to work, her mind and body shot into overdrive. Her skin tingled with sudden awareness of how close he sat to her, her lips aching for another kiss. Her brain started cataloguing how far they were from his cabin and how soon they could get there.

She'd stayed for Alanna. Mostly. But part of the reason she hadn't gotten on that plane was the man sitting next to her. Intellectually, she knew it was better to keep her distance, to focus on her sister for her remaining few days here. But her heart had other ideas. And the fact that she was still chasing after Alanna all these years later instead of moving on with her life proved that her heart almost always won.

Before she could figure out how to respond to his surprising admission, Colter spoke again. This time, his voice was all business. "Jasper says he tried to play it cool with this guy, act like all he knew was the FBI had decided it was a hoax. But he's not sure the guy bought it. So whatever he tells us today, we need to act cautiously. I don't want another situation like Henry."

Kensie's fingers instinctively grazed her still-bruised throat. It seemed to tighten at the touch. "Neither do I."

He shot a pensive glance at her, then hit the gas even harder. Before she knew it, they were pulling into the lot in front of Jasper's General Store.

Rebel ran circles around her and Colter as they made their way up to the door until finally Colter laughed and said, "Relax, girl." He looked at Kensie. "She's happy you're back."

"So am I." The words came out without thought, but they were true. Even if this turned out to be one more in a series of disappointments, she couldn't regret anything that gave her a little more time with Colter.

He held open the door for her and his gaze seemed to caress her face, as if he felt the same way.

It put a light, giddy feeling in her chest. But as she preceded him into the store and Jasper ran around the counter as soon as he spotted her, the feeling shifted into a different kind of nervous hope.

"Kensie." Jasper reached for her hands, folding them between his lean, weathered palms.

The first time she'd met him, he'd been gruff to the point of rudeness. But now he was staring at her like they were long-lost friends, and she realized her story about the day she'd watched Alanna get ripped away had touched him.

Jasper glanced up as Colter and Rebel came in behind her, nodding at them and not saying a word about Rebel being in the store. "A guy came into the store today. I recognized him from that day. And I think he might have been with the girl." His gaze went back to Kensie, his eyes wide as his words tumbled out. "I didn't recognize the girl that day, so it didn't stick, but I recognized the man."

"What?" Colter stepped closer. "You didn't mention that on the phone."

"I know. I called you as soon as he walked out and I've been trying to place him ever since. He's not a regular. Not even a semiregular. But that day wasn't the first time he's come in the store. I've seen him before. I think he could even live around here."

Kensie's heart picked up speed. If he lived around here, they had a real chance at finding him. At finding Alanna.

"I have to be honest, I probably wouldn't have connected him to that day except he was asking questions. And they were just too casual. It all felt forced, like he was desperate for the answers but didn't want me think he cared. And then I realized he'd been there. I think he walked out at the same time as the girl." He gave Kensie an apologetic look. "I can't be positive they left together that day, or even that it's your sister, but it all seems suspicious, doesn't it?"

She slid her fingers from between his palms, patting the top of one of his hands. "Yes, it does." She glanced at Colter, wondering where they went from here.

"What can you tell us about how to find him?" Colter asked.

"I walked out after him today. Tried to act all casual, but honestly, I'm not sure he bought it any more than I bought his questions just being simple curiosity. So I waved at him and grabbed the shovel I'd left out there, like that was why I'd gone out. Anyway, I saw him get into a truck, but the way he peeled away, it was like he was trying to avoid me getting a plate number."

"Which way did he go?" Colter asked.

"Now *that* I can tell you. As soon as he peeled out, I booked it upstairs. Most people don't know it, but this store has roof access. Gave me a good view of him for a while."

Jasper walked behind the counter and pulled

out a map, drawing a line away from his store and out toward what looked like nothing but forest to Kensie.

But as soon as he drew it, Colter's gaze darted up to hers, tension in the line of his jaw. "That's the same area where Henry lived. There's not much out there. It was true for Henry and it's true for whoever this guy is. It's a great place to hide."

Kensie nodded, her nerves shifting to determination. "Let's go do a little tracking."

Rebel barked her agreement.

THIS MIGHT BE HOPELESS.

Colter didn't speak the words out loud, but Kensie glanced at him as if she'd heard him anyway and shook her head.

"We need to keep going," she told him, voice tight as she leaned toward the windshield like she could lead them there by pure force of will.

It had started to snow. Big, fluffy flakes that plopped onto the windshield and slowly slid down. They were sticking, making the forest surrounding them look picturesque.

Right now, it wasn't accumulating much. But Colter knew how fast that could change out here. Although his truck was in good condition, with a nearly full tank of gas, he didn't want to take any chances. Even locals could misjudge Alaska's weather, which could turn brutal fast.

"Ten more minutes," he told Kensie, "and if the

snow hasn't stopped, we'd better turn back. We can make another trek out here tomorrow."

"But—"

"Kensie, we're three hours deep into this forest. We don't want to get trapped out here if the weather turns."

"I'll check the radar."

He glanced at her briefly, most of his attention on navigating the dirt road winding between huge fir trees. "You're probably not going to get any service. No towers out this way."

She held her phone up, testing it in different directions, then sighed. "You're right. No service."

They drove in silence for a few more minutes, but Colter could feel Kensie's tension ratcheting up. The snow remained steady, not letting up, but not getting worse, either. And still no sign of any homes.

"Do you think we missed it?" Kensie asked.

"It's possible. Usually people who live out this way don't want to be too far off of a main trail, because even these can get buried when the snow gets deep. But the road did split ten miles back. If we'd taken the other way, we would have ended up near where Henry lives. I went this route because I figured if Henry had seen your sister—if she really looks like you, the way Jasper said—Henry might have spoken up."

"Why would he? He seemed too busy trying to kill me."

He reached for her hand, squeezed it briefly. "I mean afterward. When the police were there and we were talking about your sister. If he lived near someone who looked like you, he might have put it together and said something, tried to get a little leverage."

She leaned back against her seat, twisting to face him. "Maybe we should pay him a visit and ask."

"Maybe," Colter replied, less enthusiastic about that idea. If they asked, Henry was likely to lie if he thought he could get anywhere—or just to torture Kensie, because he was a sick SOB. If he knew anything, he probably would have already volunteered it.

"Hey, what's that?" Colter slowed the truck until it was barely creeping forward as he peered through the thick trees.

"Where?"

Colter pointed. "Up ahead, at the one o'clock position, about a hundred feet ahead of us."

Kensie leaned forward again, squinting through the snow, which was beginning to fall a little faster. "I don't see anything."

He gave the truck a little more gas until Kensie exclaimed, "Oh!"

"It *is* a cabin," Colter muttered. And it was about as well hidden as you could get. If they hadn't been looking, they might have driven right past it. Positioned close enough to the road to get in and out, but far enough back to remain unseen unless you were looking. And on the other side was a mountain, so no one would notice it from that direction.

The wood cabin looked like it might have been hand constructed, but as they continued to drive forward, he realized it was a lot bigger than he'd originally thought. "You could fit a whole family in there."

His shoulders slumped as he said it. How likely was it that the person who'd grabbed Alanna lived in a cabin this big, just the two of them?

He swore as he spotted a sign at the entrance of the long unpaved drive leading up to the cabin. Two slabs of wood, one underneath the other, were staked into the ground at the entryway. The bottom one read *Trespassers will be shot*. The top one read *The Altier Family*.

"Isn't that the name of the couple Yura mentioned when we stopped by his check-cashing place?"

"What?" Kensie was still staring intently at the cabin.

"The Altiers. I'm pretty sure that's the couple who paid Henry with checks sometimes for odd jobs. It's not the guy, Kensie. Yura said this is a couple, with a bunch of kids."

Her disappointment was all over her face as she turned toward him. "Well, maybe they know who else lives around here. Let's go talk to them."

"I'm not sure that's a good idea." He pointed at the *Trespassers will be shot* sign.

As he did, he spotted a station wagon in the distance, up beside the cabin, and his heart rate doubled. Most people who lived around here drove huge trucks. The last time he'd seen a station wagon was the one that had nearly run Kensie down on the main road in Desparre.

He'd assumed it had been an accident, an idiot driving an even more idiotic car for Alaska weather. But maybe it hadn't been an accident at all. Maybe, right from the start, Kensie had been a target.

"Kensie, what did you do when you got to town? Before Rebel saved you from that car?"

She frowned at his change of topic, but answered anyway. "Not much. My plane landed and I rented a truck, then drove into town. I had to stop for directions a couple of times."

"Did you tell people about why you were here?"

"Sure. I figured I might as well, in case someone knew something. Why?"

Colter pointed through the trees again, at the station wagon. "I think that's the car that nearly ran you down. I think word got around that you were here, looking for Alanna, and someone didn't want you to find her."

Instead of fear, excitement shot across Kensie's face. "This could be it," she breathed.

"We need to go back and get the police," Colter told her, his gaze returning to the sign warning off trespassers.

"But—"

"If we've really found her, Kensie, it's not going to do her any good to get ourselves killed."

She glanced over her shoulder, back behind where Rebel sat, to where Colter had his shotgun. Her gaze lingered on it a long moment before she nodded. "You're right."

Not wanting to turn around in the Altiers' driveway and draw attention, Colter shifted into reverse, hoping there was a wide enough gap in the trees somewhere nearby for him to change direction. The truck was just starting to move backward when Kensie blurted, "Wait!"

Jamming his foot on the brake, Colter glanced back at the cabin. A group of kids had stepped outside and he scanned through them, looking for anyone who resembled Kensie.

In a way, they all did, at least from a distance. Dark hair, slight olive tone to the skin. But as he scanned them, he realized none were the right age. The youngest girl looked to be about six, then there was a boy who was probably twelve, another girl who might have been sixteen and an older boy who had to be in his early twenties. They looked like siblings.

Colter swore. "Kensie, Jasper might have seen that girl there, the oldest one. She looks a little bit like you. He might have mistaken her for Alanna."

But she was too young. It wasn't her.

From how pale she'd gone, Kensie must have realized the same thing. He reached for her hand again, all his focus on apologizing for bringing her out here for nothing.

"Colter," she breathed, pulling her hand free and pointing toward the cabin.

When he glanced back, he saw that the oldest boy was no longer there. In his place was a girl, about nineteen, with dark hair, cut to shoulder length. She had strong, thick eyebrows and lush, full lips like Kensie.

And Colter recognized her. It was the girl he'd seen in the passenger seat of the truck that had flown past him in town, when Danny had cornered Kensie. At first glance, he'd even mistaken her for Kensie.

"It's her." Kensie's voice was barely above a whisper, and he could hear the tears and joy in it at once. "It's Alanna."

She reached for the door handle and he grabbed her arm, stopping her. "Kensie, we still need the pol—"

Before he could finish his sentence, a loud *boom*, like a firecracker that had gone off way too close, split the air. Colter recognized the sound immediately: a rifle.

Chapter Nineteen

Kensie had found her. After fourteen years of searching, she'd finally found Alanna.

She was still reeling as she stared at Alanna through the forest. Her body felt frozen with disbelief, but her mind had figured it out and was screaming at her to move. To run, grab Alanna and get out of there fast.

Except Colter was yanking the truck into reverse. Then it was speeding backward fast enough to wrench Kensie hard against her belt and send Rebel sliding into her seat with a yelp.

And it still wasn't fast enough. Another *boom* blasted the air, making Kensie flinch as the front of their vehicle erupted with smoke.

"We're hit," Colter said, his voice way too calm.

Kensie stared through the smoke, realizing the blast had come from a rifle. The truck had been hit.

Panic started to break through her daze. Fear for herself, Colter and Rebel, and desperation not to lose Alanna now that she'd finally found her.

Up near the front of the cabin, the oldest boy who'd gone inside was back, pointing at their truck and yelling something. The woman next to him—in her early forties, who looked like his mother—lifted that rifle again.

"Colter—" she started to warn him.

"Get down!"

Before he'd finished speaking, Rebel's teeth were gripping the arm of her coat, tugging down until Kensie was scrunched awkwardly with her head between the seats.

But what about Colter? He was still sitting straight, jaw clenched tight as he steered the truck. A visible target.

The smoke pouring out of the engine was getting thicker and darker, and her fear intensified. "Is the engine going to blow?"

"No," Colter answered tightly, his knuckles white against the wheel as the truck sputtered, barely moving even though Kensie could see his foot jammed down on the gas.

Then, the rifle blasted again and the whole right side of the truck sank.

Kensie let out a shriek as Colter swore, struggling with the wheel as he turned the truck directly toward the trees. "She got the tire. Climb into the back seat."

"What?"

"Do it now. Hurry!"

Hands shaking, she fumbled with her seatbelt

as he fought with the wheel, until finally she realized what he was doing. Angling the truck the other way, so his side was facing the rifle and giving her more protection.

"Colter—"

"I'm right behind you. Go!"

Kensie launched herself into the back, squashed up next to Rebel, who'd been smart enough to get down on the floor behind her seat.

Colter twisted, jamming himself between the front seats. His shoulders were too broad and he seemed to get stuck, but he stretched his arm out and grabbed his shotgun.

Kensie tried to press even closer to Rebel, making room, and Rebel squeezed tighter into the door without complaint. "Get back here," she demanded.

But Colter was going the other way. He stayed low, but he shimmied back into the front.

She yanked on the sleeve of his coat, even as he popped open the glove compartment, grabbing a box of shells. He jammed several into the shotgun, stuffed the rest into his pocket and told her, "When I tell you to, open that door and make a run for the trees."

"Colter—"

"Get ready," he barked, lifting the shotgun.

There was another ear-splitting blast and the windshield shattered, spraying glass into the truck. It pricked her arms and Kensie shrieked.

Then she gagged as heavy, dark smoke rushed into the cabin.

Colter. Had he been hit?

Kensie twisted, lifting her head, trying to get a better look at him. Almost instantly his hand was there, shoving her head back down. But not before she saw two things. Colter wasn't hit. And the woman who'd been shooting at them was now running toward the truck, rifle still raised.

"Colter," she warned, choking on the smoke, her words coming out gravelly, in a voice that didn't sound like it belonged to her. "She's coming!"

"Plan hasn't changed," he said gruffly, calmly. "Grab the handle. You're about to go."

"But—"

"On the count of three! One, two, three, go!"

Heart thundering, pounding hard enough to hurt her chest—or maybe that was the smoke she was inhaling—Kensie shoved open the door.

"Go, Rebel! Trees!" Colter yelled.

Rebel shot out the door, and Kensie scrambled after her even as her mind screamed for Colter.

She heard the blast of a shotgun, once, twice, as she choked on the fresh air, as she took huge, desperate strides. She ran in the path Rebel made, the dog easily outpacing her.

"Colter!" She thought she screamed for him, but maybe it was only in her mind as another *boom* seemed to make the ground shake.

Then pain raced up her leg, intense as fire, and Kensie crashed to the ground.

Kensie was down.

Colter's whole world narrowed to just her form, falling into the snow. The edges of his vision darkened as he gasped for breath, and the blast of a sniper rifle went off somewhere above him. Then there was a crushing weight on his chest, Rebel's paws slamming into him. He barely had time to register any of it before he was falling, falling...

Colter's hands darted out, reaching for something, anything to break his fall. The shotgun he was holding smacked the truck seat and smashed his fingers. But it made no sense. There was no truck here, only debris. Only the blasted-apart remains of a transport vehicle, the unexpected grave of too many soldiers.

"Colter!"

Kensie's panicked voice broke through his confusion, pulled him out of that nightmare overseas where he'd lost all his brothers. Brought him back to her.

Only he wasn't with her. She was shot and he was inside a truck that was rapidly filling with smoke. And although he'd fired at the woman with the rifle, it was too hard to see through the black smoke. He had no idea if he'd hit her.

Move, his brain screamed. Colter gasped for breath, trying to subdue the panic as he choked on smoke. From a distance, Rebel's bark reached him, as if she was urging him to hurry.

It was a tight fit between the seats, but even with the smoke obscuring everything, he didn't want to make too big a target. He was no good to Kensie if he was dead.

Colter shoved and twisted, finally managing to get his shoulders between the seats. He dragged the shotgun behind him, the only weapon he had. At the open back door, he paused, getting a better view of the cabin.

The woman was still standing, but she was no longer shooting at them. Instead, she was taking cover behind the door, pulling the youngest two kids with her. Still standing in the yard was the oldest boy, who was holding a pistol, taking aim at Kensie.

"No!" His voice mingled with someone else's and before Colter could launch free of the vehicle, the girl they thought was Alanna tackled the boy.

Colter didn't wait. Leaving his cane behind and gripping the shotgun carefully, he darted out of the truck, dropping to his haunches beside Kensie. Her calf was bleeding, but it wasn't the kind of wound made by a rifle. It could have been ricochet, but most likely, it was a bullet from the pistol.

Relief gave him his first full breath. The cold air hurt, but seemed to clear some of the smoke from his lungs. Keeping hold of the shotgun while lifting her wasn't easy, but he knew they were probably going to need a weapon. His right leg trembled, pain burning his thigh, and he prayed it wouldn't give out on him.

Thankfully it held as he draped Kensie over his left shoulder and started to run. "Go, girl!" he told Rebel, who was ahead of them, in the cover of the trees.

His dog took off, darting from one tree to the next, a blur of brown and black fur. She left an obvious trail of paw prints in the snow and Colter knew he would be doing the same. They'd be easy to track.

There was only one main road in and out of the area, the one they'd come in on. They'd be easy targets there, but he wasn't sure this was much better. He hadn't given Rebel instructions other than to run, which was all they could do right now. There was no time to strategize with a family carrying weapons potentially right behind them. But they were heading deeper into the wilderness, toward the edge of a mountain, farther away from help or shelter.

His leg throbbed, shaking each time he put weight on it, especially at the pace he was going. Every twenty feet, Rebel stopped, glancing back at them, waiting for him to catch up.

Kensie was light. He'd once run with a fellow soldier, someone double her weight, over his shoulder for two miles. But that was before his leg had been irreparably damaged. Now it was all he could manage to keep his grip on her and the shotgun, keep his feet from sliding out from under him. It got even worse once the ground started to slope downward.

He wanted to glance behind him, see if the woman with the rifle or the boy with the pistol were following. But he knew if he did, he'd lose his balance. With each step, the slope was getting steeper. He wanted to double back, go the other way. Seek higher ground, the way he'd been trained. But there was no chance of that. It was too steep now, and it would take them right back toward the Altiers.

He needed a plan, because they'd managed to head right down the side of a mountain, when he'd hoped there'd be a straight route alongside the edge. Anyone standing at the top of the mountain would have a good view of them, no matter the trees. Then again, the trees were getting thicker the farther down they went. And a moving target wasn't easy to hit. He needed to move faster.

"I can run!"

Kensie's voice penetrated his thoughts and he realized she'd been repeating it, her words muffled against his back. But he also knew it was wishful thinking on her part. She'd taken a bullet to the calf. She might be able to push herself for a while, but he didn't want to test that theory now. Not while they were still so close to the cabin.

He didn't respond. He couldn't. With every step, the mountain was getting steeper, until he found himself leaning backward for leverage, slowing his steps so they wouldn't both go tumbling down. Up ahead even Rebel had slowed, and he realized she, too, had started to limp. Her back leg was acting up because she'd pushed it too hard.

Colter wanted to use the trees for support, grab them to slow his descent. But he couldn't, not with Kensie slung over his left shoulder and the shotgun barely grasped in his right hand.

The cold burned his throat and lungs and made his eyes water. The tears seemed to freeze on his cheeks, the wind brutal as the slope continued to get steeper. It was too steep. He slowed even more, taking slightly sideways steps, back and forth, to help him navigate down.

Rebel was handling the terrain better, but she'd looped back for him, sticking by his side. He wanted to tell her to go ahead, but he couldn't manage to get the command out. And he wasn't sure she'd obey it even if he did, especially when his bad leg buckled slightly, and his foot slid dangerously forward. He managed to catch himself by angling his free shoulder right into the trunk of a tree. The branches whipped against his face, against Kensie's legs hanging over his chest. It ripped the shotgun out of his hand, sent it tumbling down the mountain, bouncing off trees as it crashed downward. The path he and Kensie would take if he slipped again.

Keeping his shoulder pressed into the tree, Colter regained his footing. Lungs screaming, heart thundering, he stopped, finally glancing back. Scanning the ridge of the mountain, he saw nothing. No woman with a rifle, no boy with a pistol.

He strained to hear over the racing of his heart, but he couldn't make out the sound of an engine, either. Not a truck or even a snowmobile, which would be much more agile to come after them and which the Altiers surely had, living so far from resources.

"Rebel," he wheezed, tapping his thigh.

His dog scooted under the tree with them and Colter eased down, lowering Kensie off his shoulders. Setting her down made his legs tremble violently. When he had her on the ground, he allowed himself to slide down, too, praying he'd be able to get back up.

"Are you okay?" she asked, her eyes huge, before he could ask her the same thing.

"Let me see your leg," he said instead of answering.

She scooted around, grimacing as she lifted her left calf onto his lap so he could get a look at it.

Her jeans were saturated with blood below the knee. The bullet had ripped a hole through her pants that he didn't want to open further in this weather. But he could see the swollen, damaged skin that was exposed, and the injury was still pumping out blood.

Colter probed it as gently as he could. There was no exit wound. Probably because of the distance, maybe the angle. He couldn't tell where the bullet was, if it had lodged right below the entrance or if it had ricocheted around inside of her, redirected by bone until it made a mess.

He had basic medic training, but he didn't have the supplies to deal with a bullet wound. All he could do was stop the bleeding and get her to a hospital as soon as possible.

The second he peeled off his winter coat, his body tensed up as the cold penetrated deeper. Ignoring it, he peeled off his shirt, then the undershirt he wore beneath. Swearing, he quickly pulled his shirt back on, zipping his coat over it. Then he wrapped the undershirt around Kensie's leg, knotting it tightly enough to make her yelp.

"Sorry. I've got to stop the bleeding."

Thankfully, it did stop. Not instantly, but his shirt went from white to a pale pink and then didn't change. He prayed it would stay that way if she had to run on it. Because he wasn't sure he could carry her out of here.

He wanted to stay under this tree, rest a while. But as Kensie traced a finger over the welts on his face from the branches, he peeked out from underneath the tree. Still no sign of the family on the top of the mountain. But the longer they stayed in one spot without moving, the more the cold would seep into them. The more likely they were to slowly die from exposure.

"Do you see them?" Kensie whispered, reminding him of the problem of running: the possibility that one or both of them would get shot.

"No."

"They're not coming after us." Kensie's shoulders slumped and moisture filled her eyes. "They're running. They know we found Alanna, and now they have time to disappear."

Chapter Twenty

It was starting to get dark.

Kensie peered up at the sky for a split second and lost her balance. Her arms darted out, seeking something to grip, and found a tree branch on the left. It slowed her, but then the branch snapped and her feet slid again, her boots not getting enough traction in the snow.

It had been falling faster since they'd taken shelter briefly under the fir tree where Colter had wrapped her leg. She'd suggested waiting to see if it slowed, but Colter had insisted they keep moving.

He'd looked worried then. He looked even more worried now as his arm shot out in front of her, giving her something to hold.

She grabbed on with both hands. He grunted as he stiffened his arm, stopping her downward slide.

"Sorry," she wheezed. It hurt to talk. Colter had pulled her hood over her head earlier, knotting it tight, reducing her peripheral vision but helping her retain heat. Supposedly.

But since they'd left the shelter of the fir tree, the cold had seemed to invade her from the inside out, settling in her lungs and even her bones. Her left leg throbbed and the shirt Colter had wrapped around it was now bright red. She was unbearably tired and scared that the exhaustion was less from the trek and more from loss of blood.

She had no idea how long it had been since they'd run from the cabin, just that it was long enough for the sun to settle low in the sky. The three of them were still picking their way down the mountain. She and Colter were using the trees for support. Rebel was better at keeping her balance, but even she was sliding periodically and she'd started favoring her injured back leg.

She and Colter were both limping badly. She knew Colter hated himself for not being able to carry her, so she was doing her best not to show how much her leg hurt. But the truth was, the pain was more excruciating than anything she'd ever experienced.

With every step, no matter how gentle, a jolt went up her leg, all the way to her hip. More and more, she felt like she might throw up from it, so she clamped her jaw tight and tried to focus on each new goal. First the big fir tree fifty feet ahead of them, then the boulder twenty-five feet away. Now it was just getting from one tree to the next, simply taking each step without slipping and tumbling down the mountainside.

The warmer coat Colter had made her buy was back in her luggage, in his ruined truck. She was wearing the one she'd arrived in, which could handle Chicago's tough wind chill, but not this. Not being stranded on the side of a mountain, only the trees blocking the sudden gusts of ice-cold wind. Not the dampness seeping into her bones as the snowflakes soaked through her jeans, slid into her gloves whenever she grabbed a tree branch for support.

"Hang on," Colter said.

Kensie grabbed the nearest tree, sagging against it as Rebel pressed close to her side. Kensie suspected it was to lend her warmth, but even the dog was starting to look cold. Kensie's eyes slid shut and she tipped her head, resting it, too, against the tree. It felt iced over and it soaked her hood even more, but right now, she didn't care. More than anything, she craved sleep.

When she heard Colter swear, it was harder than it should have been to open her eyes again. "What 'sit?" she slurred. Her mind felt foggy, but not so foggy she didn't realize that was a bad sign.

Hypothermia did that. Kensie focused on her fingers and toes, trying to decide if she could feel them. It was strange that she couldn't tell. She tried to wiggle her toes and almost lost her balance. "What is it?" she asked again, enunciating carefully.

Lines raked Colter's forehead and she wanted

to smooth them away, wanted to make the worry in his sky-blue eyes disappear. But it was all she could do to stay on her feet.

"I thought we might have gone far enough to get service."

For a long moment, his words made no sense. Then she glanced at his hands, which were stuffing his cell phone into his pocket. Despite having warm gloves, his hands were bright red, the fingertips an alarming white. As soon as he'd returned the cell phone to his pocket, he shoved his hands back into his gloves, rubbing them together.

"We walked that far?" she asked, happy she wasn't slurring anymore. At least she didn't think so.

"No. We're headed sort of perpendicular to the path we took to the cabin, down the mountain. We're not going toward Desparre, but there's another town out this way. It looked like I might have a signal, but the call kept dropping. I tried texting 911 anyway."

"How will they find us?" Her words ran together, barely comprehensible, and Kensie tried to focus, tried to get her sluggish mind to connect properly with her mouth. She tried it again, and this time he understood.

"We've got to keep moving."

She whimpered, the idea of continuing on any farther seeming impossible.

In response, Colter slid closer, wrapped an arm

around her waist, taking some of her weight even as his jaw clenched.

The sight gave her strength and she stiffened, took a deep, cold breath. If she gave up, she knew he'd carry her as far as he could. But what if her extra weight was the difference between his making it or dying on this mountain? "I'm okay," she told him, surprised when her voice came out determined and clear.

She had to make it. For Colter and Rebel, who'd put their lives on hold to help her. And for Alanna, who might already be packed up in the Altiers's car, on her way to some other out-of-the-way town, where she might stay hidden for another fourteen years. If Kensie died here, no one would know the truth about who had taken her sister.

That wasn't going to happen.

She stiffened her shoulders and took a step forward. Her injured leg gave out on her and she hit the ground hard, her head smacking the dirt and snow. The world rotated in a dizzying swirl and then she was sliding, picking up speed as she went.

Reaching out, Kensie grappled for anything. Her hand snagged a low-lying branch and she held tight. Her back arched up off the ground, then came back down, but somehow she held on, the image of Colter's worried face giving her strength. She couldn't die like this. She couldn't give him one more loss to grieve, one more reason to blame himself when it wasn't his fault.

It took her a minute to realize she'd stopped moving, but she didn't let go of the branch, because it was still steep. Then Colter came sliding down next to her, half out of control, Rebel right behind him.

"You okay?" Colter's voice was panicked.

She tipped her head back toward him and tried to smile. Tried to reassure him without words that she was all right, that she wasn't giving up. That they'd make it.

But the truth was, she wasn't sure. Because when she tried to push herself to her feet, no matter how much she gritted her teeth, her leg kept giving out on her.

"It's okay," Colter said, bending next to her.

Then she was up, dangling over his shoulder again. Tears spilled over, even as she tried to stop them, knowing the moisture was just going to freeze on her skin.

Colter grunted, using tree branches for leverage, his right leg dragging slightly behind him. Keeping pace beside him, Rebel pressed close against him and Kensie saw the dog's back left leg was barely taking weight.

She didn't need to be able to see down the mountain to know they were far from the bottom. Far from civilization or help.

Dread filled her, bone-deep and exhausting.

They weren't going to make it. And it didn't matter if she begged. Colter would never leave her behind to save himself.

But if they were going to die out here, she wanted him to know how much his help meant to her. How much meeting him had changed her life. Had changed the way she thought about herself, the way she thought about what she wanted.

Meeting him had changed everything.

She'd been lying to herself, thinking she was halfway in love with him. When it came to Colter, there was no halfway. She was straight-up in love with the man. And after everything he'd been through—all the loss and guilt—she wanted him to know he was still worthy of love.

Yes, he was damaged, but so was she. And damaged was far different from broken.

Sucking in a breath full of frigid air, Kensie projected, wanting to be sure her words weren't lost on the wind. "I love you, Colter."

WAS HE STARTING to hallucinate?

Colter had wanted to give his coat—better suited for the freezing climate—to Kensie hours ago, but he'd known he wouldn't survive without it. And with her injured leg, he wasn't sure she'd be able to make it out on her own. Her makeshift bandage had been saturated with blood more than an hour ago, the wound bleeding freely again.

He'd tightened it repeatedly, stemming the flow more than once. But it always started up again.

Even with his better gear, he knew they were both in serious danger of frostbite and hypothermia. Every breath hurt his lungs and his fingers had felt clumsy and uncoordinated on the too-tiny numbers of his phone. Maybe his mind was going, too. It was the only explanation for the auditory hallucination he'd just experienced, Kensie saying she loved him.

He snorted. Maybe in his wildest dreams.

But then he heard it again, and there was no denying it was her beautiful voice speaking the words, even though her voice was rough from the chill. Joy filled his heart so fast it actually hurt, but worry followed immediately.

She thought they were going to die. It was the only reason she'd admit something like that.

He wanted to say it right back to her. The thought shocked him, made him set his right leg down crooked, twisting it sideways. He slipped, but righted himself quickly, even as it registered that he hadn't felt pain like he should have. His body was shutting down.

Or maybe the joy of her words was just overriding any pain.

He glanced at Rebel, sticking to his painfully slow pace beside him. She was struggling, too, whimpering every once in a while when she put weight on that back leg. "I'm sorry, girl," he whispered.

Louder, to Kensie, he said, "You're just scared. We're going to be fine. Save your strength."

But his mind was screaming at him to say it back. He loved her.

The very idea was shocking. He hadn't thought he was capable of loving anyone new. Hadn't thought his heart had any room left in it after the loss of his brothers.

He loved his family, loved Rebel. But that was all he could handle. A woman like Kensie deserved so much more than he could give her.

And yet...he wanted to give her the world. He wanted to stand beside her, not just when they made it off this mountain, but years beyond. Wanted to experience a life with her, have children with her.

The thought was a betrayal of the promise he'd made that day when he'd woken up in the hospital and the doctors had finally admitted to him what he already knew in his heart. They were gone, all of them. He was the only survivor.

He'd looked up at the ceiling and promised never to forget them, swore he'd bide his time until he joined them. He'd never felt suicidal and yet, for the past year, he hadn't really wanted to live. Probably the only reason he'd come this far—pushed through the agony of his surgeries and the long recovery—was Rebel. His partner. His family.

But somehow, in the past four days, Kensie had become his family, too. He loved her.

He loved her.

It didn't even seem possible in such a short time, but he couldn't deny the emotion rising up in him. The protectiveness, the desperation to save her, no matter what it cost him.

"I love you."

For a second, he thought he'd spoken his thoughts aloud. Then, he realized she was repeating herself.

"Kensie, we're going to make it," he told her. "I know you're scared, but you have to believe." When she tried to speak again, he cut her off, lungs burning as he kept pressing forward, one slow step at a time. "Tell you what. When we make it out of here safely, if you still want to, you can tell me. Okay?"

Getting so many words out made his lungs scream, but he had to do it. If she really did love him, maybe it would help her hold on. Even if his leg gave out, maybe he could get her far enough. He'd tell Rebel to lead her out. His dog wouldn't want to leave him, but he knew she'd come to love Kensie as much as he had. And Rebel was tough, just like Kensie. With a break, with Rebel by her side, Kensie could push through. The two of them could make it. He just had to get them as far as he could.

But his leg was slowing him down more with every step. The pain was back now, the numbness from before gone, and he wasn't sure if that was a good sign or a bad one. Because he could barely feel the rest of his body. He had no idea how he was keeping hold of Kensie, but he knew if he adjusted his grip at all, it would break.

He'd never felt this much agony in his life, not even when he'd woken on that airplane, with a piece of metal slicing straight through his thigh. His face burned, like he'd scalded it. His lungs felt frozen, as if they had to chip free of his ribs with every breath. And his leg was the worst. It shook so much he knew it was only a matter of time before it gave out entirely. And each step sent pain from his knee up to his hip and then back down, as if that metal was still impaled there.

He wasn't going to make it. He was going to fail her, like he'd failed his brothers. They were going to die out here.

"You've made me believe I'm worthy of a life that's truly mine." Kensie's voice cut through his thoughts, a strange raspy croak that sounded nothing like her normal voice. "I want you to believe what I already know. That you're worthy of a good life, too. Even if it's not with me."

She thought he didn't want a life with her? He didn't have the energy to correct her, but keeping her talking wasn't a bad idea. It would keep her awake. Falling asleep was a quicker trip to hypothermia.

But she was wrong. He wasn't worthy. His right

leg was failing him. He couldn't even lift it anymore, just slide it forward and pray he didn't lose traction and send them both tumbling down the mountain.

He glanced at Rebel and her soft brown eyes stared back at him, weary but determined. Rebel was still going on force of will and love for him and Kensie. She'd never give up, his dog, his partner.

In that instant, a new kind of strength filled him. A strength that wasn't his own.

He glanced at the sky and he could almost feel his Marine brothers, watching over him, helping him. "Thank you," he rasped.

Then he heard the most beautiful sound he'd ever heard in his life. The familiar *whomp whomp whomp* of a helicopter.

He lifted his gaze skyward once more and there it was, circling overhead. A spotlight shot past them, then darted back. They'd been found.

Colter's leg gave out and he collapsed.

Chapter Twenty-One

Colter woke with a start in an unfamiliar hospital bed. The beeping of the heart monitor next to him accelerated as the past few hours came back to him. "Kensie!"

"She's okay," a nurse reassured him.

Colter took a few deep breaths, getting his heart rate under control. This had happened several times already.

The helicopter he'd spotted from the mountain was a police chopper, sent out after his text to 911 had gone through. It hadn't been able to set down for them on the wooded mountainside, so Colter had forced himself up. Beside him, Kensie had managed to do the same with Rebel pressed against her side. Together, the three of them had limped as far as they could, until finally a rescue team met them.

Now they were here, getting checked out. As hard as he'd tried to stay awake, Colter kept drifting off to sleep.

Beside him, Rebel pushed wearily to her feet and the nurse gave his dog a stern look.

"She shouldn't be here." The nurse repeated the same thing she said every time he woke.

"She's my service dog."

The nurse grunted, clearly not believing him. But hospital administration had—or, at least, that's what he'd assumed, until a doctor had winked at him then bent down and checked Rebel's leg, too. The doc had said his wife was military and he knew a soldier dog when he saw one.

Rebel seemed to like that and let the doctor examine her. He'd put ointment and gauze over each of her paws and then gently wrapped her leg. Thankfully, she hadn't torn anything, just aggravated the old injury. It just needed time, the doctor told him. Much like Colter's own leg.

They'd stripped off his wet clothes and soaked his hands, feet and nose—which all had minor frostbite—in warm water. Now his hands and feet were bare, wrapped in gauze, and he was in a hospital gown.

He knew Kensie had also suffered from frostbite, that she'd been experiencing hypothermia. But they'd assured him she would survive, then rushed her off to surgery to remove the bullet from her leg. That was the last he'd seen her.

Colter glanced at the clock on the wall, trying to remember what time they'd arrived. "What's taking so long?" he asked the nurse.

"We're making sure we address everything," she replied, a little more patiently than she'd responded to Rebel's presence. "She'll be okay." Then she glanced over at the door. "You've got visitors."

His gaze shot up. Rebel's did, too, surely expecting the same thing he did. To see Kensie standing there, smiling tiredly. Instead, he discovered a pair of police officers.

He didn't know either of them. They were wearing uniforms from a town northeast of Desparre, closer to where the helicopter had found him, Kensie and Rebel.

The pair stepped into his room, both serious cops who looked like they'd been on the force a long time. The nurse left, closing the door behind her, and Colter's heart pounded. "Did you find them?"

When the rescue team had arrived, Kensie's first words had been about her sister. She'd been frantic and desperate, barely making sense, so Colter had filled in as best he could with aching lungs and a body that wanted to just lie down and sleep.

He'd been asking for updates every time he woke, but no one seemed to know anything.

"We sent a tactical team out to the cabin," one of the officers replied. "It was partially cleared out. We're tracking the Altiers now. We've talked to the nearest neighbors—a couple of miles away—

and learned it's a family of seven. The parents and five children. The neighbor confirmed the oldest girl is named Alanna."

The news sent a shock through Colter, even though Kensie's reaction when she'd seen the girl had already told him it was her.

"Our team is still searching. We'll let you know as soon as we find them."

The officer spoke with confidence, as if locating the Altier family was a foregone conclusion, but Colter's shoulders slumped. They'd managed to keep Alanna hidden for so long. What if they got away again? How would Kensie survive coming so close, only to lose her sister once more?

Colter's heart ached for her. He'd do anything he could to help her, assuming she wanted his help. But in all the time since they'd arrived, while he was worrying about how she was faring, he hadn't been able to stop thinking about one other thing.

When they'd gotten to safety, she hadn't repeated her words from the mountain. She hadn't repeated that she loved him.

He wanted to say the words back to her anyway. But should he? Or should he give her a clean break, let her focus on her family, on trying to make it whole again?

A shriek outside his door jolted him out of his thoughts and he realized the officers had left. Rebel jumped up at the sound, recognizing the voice, even though it didn't sound quite normal. Kensie.

Together, they moved as quickly as they could to the door and Colter flung it open, ready to handle whatever threat faced her. Instead, he saw a different pair of officers walking down the hall, Alanna between them.

Kensie was in the hallway, too, in a hospital gown, her leg wrapped up. She limped awkwardly toward the trio, not even noticing him as she breathed, "Alanna?"

"Kensie!" the girl replied, racing toward her sister and wrapping her in a hug.

AFTER FOURTEEN LONG YEARS, Kensie was finally hugging her sister again.

It didn't feel real. The last time she'd wrapped her arms around Alanna, she'd had to bend down to reach the five-year-old. She'd buried her head in her sister's unruly curls, breathed in that little-kid scent of sugar and dirt that she still smelled whenever she thought of Alanna.

Now her sister was nineteen and only two inches shorter than Kensie. Her hair was thick and straight, cut in a blunt line at her shoulders, highlighting the elegant lines of her face.

Kensie pulled back, holding Alanna at arm's length to get a good look at her.

"We still look like sisters," Alanna whispered. Her voice was different, too, and yet a hint of the five-year-old was still there. Tears filled Kensie's eyes and she swiped them away, not wanting to miss a single detail of her sister's face, all grown up.

They *did* look like sisters. Kensie's hair was longer, but if they twined strands together, Kensie doubted they'd be able to tell whose was whose. Alanna's eyes were a darker brown, closer to Flynn's than Kensie's, but she and her sister had the same long eyelashes, the same strong eyebrows. People would have known they were family at a single glance.

What would it have been like to grow up with Alanna? With eight years between them, they never would have been in school together, but Kensie would have wanted to be her protector. Just like she had when she was thirteen.

"I'm so sorry," Kensie whispered back, remembering that moment in their front yard, the defining moment in her life. When she'd read a book while Alanna had run around the yard, too close to the street. When a car had sped up to their curb, slammed to a stop, and the man inside it yanked Alanna away from them.

Alanna took her hands. "It's not your fault."

Kensie burst into tears. It hurt her lungs and her face, which she'd only started to feel again in the past hour. Wiping her tears away with her arm so she could keep hold of her sister's hands, Kensie gave a shaking smile. "I've missed you so much."

From the corner of her eye, she spotted Colter and Rebel, standing in the doorway of a hospital room. They were sliding quietly backward, obviously trying to let her and Alanna have a private reunion.

But there'd have been no reunion at all if it weren't for the two of them. Keeping her right hand gripped in Alanna's, she turned her head and held out her left for Colter.

He seemed a little unsure, but Rebel limped over immediately, pushing her way in between Kensie and Alanna and making Alanna laugh.

Kensie's heart felt so full at the sound. As her sister petted Rebel, Kensie stretched her hand out farther, silently imploring Colter.

When he stepped carefully toward her on bandaged feet and placed his hand in hers, she squeezed tight. She never wanted to let go of any of them, ever again.

She wasn't sure how long they stood there, in the hospital hallway, huddled together and smiling at each other, until Alanna suggested, "Let's sit."

The pain in her leg had actually been forgotten, seeing Alanna safe, but now it returned in a wave of agony. She wasn't supposed to be standing on it yet, let alone walking.

They must have been quite a sight, limping into her hospital room. Once she was seated, Colter beside her, Alanna on the empty bed across from them and Rebel on the ground between them, Kensie asked, "What happened all these years, Alanna?"

As soon as the words were out, she wanted to call them back. What if her sister had been terribly abused? What if it hurt her too much to talk about it? Was Kensie prepared to hear what Alanna had endured?

Colter's fingers slid through hers, squeezing gently, lending her strength, and Kensie tried to stay strong for Alanna.

But her sister shook her head. "It's not what you're thinking. They were...good to me."

"*Good* to you? They *kidnapped* you, Alanna! They stole you from us for fourteen years!"

"I know. And all that time, I tried so hard not to forget you and Flynn, and Mom and Dad. I tried so hard to protect my memories. It wasn't easy. I was five. But I still have good memories. I was one of the lucky ones."

"What do you mean?"

"You saw them, right? At the cabin?"

The other kids. Kensie had assumed they were the Altiers's own children, that only Alanna had been abducted. Realization made the blood seem to drain from her body. "They were all kidnapped?"

"Yeah. The younger two don't remember their birth families at all. Sydney—she's twelve—remembers best. She was the oldest when they took her and I guess they learned from that, because they started picking younger kids. Johnny—my older brother—he was five, like me. He barely remembers his birth family. It's why they've been able to mold him so much. It's why he shot at you. To protect the family."

Kensie swallowed back her instant response. Johnny wasn't her older brother. *Flynn* was her older brother. And she and Flynn and their parents weren't Alanna's *birth* family. They were simply her family.

Colter pulled her hand into his lap, stroking her palm gently, like he could read her mind. Across from them, Alanna sighed.

"I guess it's hard to understand," she said. "But I lived with the Altiers for fourteen years, most of my life. They picked kids who looked like them. They wanted a family and couldn't have one, so they kidnapped kids. They treated us well, never hurt any of us. They wanted us to be happy, but the way we lived—it was like kids probably did a long time ago. We worked hard, all of us. We lived off the land. We were all homeschooled. And we moved around. A lot. Especially at the beginning. Until eventually we came here. I guess they felt Alaska was safe, because we built the cabin. We finally stayed in one place."

"You were happy?" The question was hard to get out, because she hoped her sister would say yes, but some part of her felt like it was wrong for Alanna to have been happy with her kidnappers.

Alanna's gaze dropped to her lap and she fiddled with a worn gold and garnet ring on her right hand. It looked like an antique, something that would get passed down in families. But it hadn't come from the Morgans.

"Mostly." She met Kensie's gaze again, her eyes imploring Kensie to understand. "I never forgot you, Kensie. I never forgot any of you. I wanted to come home. I tried not to let them know, but I always wanted to come home."

"And at that store, you finally had a chance to write a note without being seen?" Kensie asked, trying to contain her emotions. There were so many. Happiness at having Alanna back, regret at missing most of her childhood, anger that the people who'd stolen her had pretended *they* were her family, relief that Alanna hadn't been hurt or abused.

Alanna bit her lip. "Sort of. I—"

When Alanna looked like she might cry, Kensie assured her, "It's okay. Whatever it is, you can tell me. We're sisters."

Alanna smiled. It trembled on her lips, her eyes still watery, but it was fueled by happiness. Kensie knew because it looked just like her own smile.

Happiness burst inside of her at sharing that with her sister. In that moment, she knew whatever Alanna had been through, whatever Alanna needed to help her move forward, they could do it together. They could rebuild their family. Finally.

"I had chances before. I was allowed to go places. I mean, they watched me, but they trusted me, too, once I'd been with them for a while. It's just that..."

"What?" Kensie whispered.

"I love them."

The words made Kensie's chest hurt, made her whole body tense up. But she tried not to show it.

"I'm sorry," Alanna said. "I know that has to be hard to hear. But they raised me. I knew they'd kidnapped me, but they treated me well. They took care of me and over the years, I just—"

"It's okay," Kensie assured her. It *was* hard to hear, but she understood. And although she didn't want to owe the Altiers anything, she was grateful they'd given Alanna a good childhood.

"But last month, Johnny started talking about wanting to get married. He'd met this girl and he was so excited about adding to our family and I just... I realized if I didn't try, I'd never get any milestones like that with you, Flynn, Mom or Dad."

"Were they mad when they learned what you'd done?" Kensie asked, not wanting to think about what the rest of her life might have been like if Alanna hadn't taken that risk.

"Yeah. They thought we'd lucked out when the FBI called it a hoax, but then they said you'd come to town. They were talking about leaving. I convinced them to let me go into town, to just see it one more time. It was the only place I'd lived for more than a year—except back in Illinois with you. Da—Mr. Altier took me into town late at night, figuring not many people would be around."

The day she'd followed Henry. He must have gone the other way, down the alley and back toward town, instead of into the storage units, like she'd thought. But without knowing it, he'd led her right to Alanna.

Alanna burst into tears. "When that man attacked you in the parking lot, I thought I'd gotten you killed."

Kensie shoved to her feet, her leg screaming as she put weight on it, and folded her sister into a hug. Hopefully just one of many, many hugs to come. "No. You saved me. You and Colter and Rebel. You saved me."

"Alanna Altier?"

Kensie's head swiveled at the question and she saw a doctor waiting in the doorway. She wanted to correct him about her sister's name, but kept quiet. There would be time for that. Right now was a time to reunite.

"I need you to come with me so we can make sure you're okay."

"I'm fine," Alanna said, her arms still looped loosely around Kensie.

"I'm sure you are, but this won't take long," the doctor insisted.

Alanna looked at Kensie and she nodded. "I'll be waiting for you," Kensie promised.

As the doctor led her sister into another room, Kensie sank onto the bed Alanna had just vacated, staring at Colter as disbelief and joy mingled. "I can't believe any of this is real. I can't believe we found her."

Colter smiled back at her, the sight of it already so familiar and comforting. "Believe it," he told her. "This is your new normal."

"I've got to call my family," Kensie said, even as her mind screamed that she wanted *him* to be part of her new normal, too.

"I can go," Colter said, standing. "Let you call them."

"No." Kensie reached out for him and he let her pull him closer. Her heart beat a frantic, frightened tempo as she stared into his eyes, wanting him to see the truth of her words as she spoke them.

Obviously sensing something important was happening, Rebel scooted closer, pressing against Colter's side.

"I meant what I said on the mountain," Kensie blurted before she could lose her nerve. "I know it's fast and I know it's not what you were looking for, but I can't help it. I love you."

She had to tell him. He'd done so much for her. He'd lost so much in the past year. Even if he couldn't love her back, she wanted him to know that he was worthy of someone giving him everything they had.

She expected his face to twist with regret and discomfort, but instead he smiled. It started out slow and sexy, putting crinkles beside his eyes. Then it burst wide and Kensie's heart seemed to do the same.

"I love you, too, Kensie."

Epilogue

His journey was coming to an end. He hoped.

Colter stared up at the apartment complex across from the lake, frozen in place. The wind coming off the water was cold, but nothing compared to the brutal weather Desparre was getting right now. Beside him, Rebel nudged his leg with her head, as if to say *get moving*.

Colter laughed. "Be patient, girl."

It had been a month since he'd seen Kensie. He'd dropped her and Alanna at the airport, watched as Alanna stared nervously up at the sky. She'd never been on a plane. The people who'd raised her since she was five were in custody and she hadn't wanted to leave behind the siblings she'd grown up with. But they all had families, too, people who'd been waiting for them, praying for this day to come.

Kensie had stared back at him, a smile trembling on her lips and tears in her eyes. She needed to go, needed to help Alanna transition back into a life she barely remembered. Needed to be with her family as they all reunited.

And his place was in Alaska. Over the past year, it had truly become his home. The noise of a city brought on unexpected panic, while the quiet solitude of his cabin soothed his soul. Gave him a little peace.

He hadn't wanted to let her go, but he couldn't go with her.

The truth was, they hardly knew each other. A long-distance relationship from Alaska to Chicago seemed a little crazy, but they'd vowed to give it a shot.

But over the past month, he'd realized it wasn't right. He couldn't move on like this. There was still too much baggage from his past weighing him down.

So for the past three weeks he'd been lying to Kensie. He'd pretended he was still in Alaska whenever they talked. But the slightly guarded tone her voice had taken on lately told him she suspected something wasn't right. Or maybe she was starting to have second thoughts about their arrangement, too.

Swallowing his nerves, Colter tapped his leg for Rebel, but she was already up and moving. He had to follow her into the complex. He almost forgot to use the cane he'd brought along for show as they hurried through the doors. He'd done his research beforehand—this apartment complex didn't allow pets.

The guy sitting behind the security desk frowned and Colter leaned heavily on the cane. "Sorry. I forgot her service vest."

The guy looked like he was going to argue, so Colter rushed to the elevator, ignoring the man's calls to sign in. The doors slid closed behind him and Rebel before anyone could stop them.

As the elevator rose, so did Colter's stress level. He hated enclosed spaces, especially ones made of metal. Closing his eyes, he breathed slowly in and out through his nose as Rebel pressed hard against his side.

"Thanks, girl," he said as the elevator dinged and the doors opened, letting them off on the fourth floor. Kensie's floor.

Swinging the cane back and forth as he walked, Colter followed Rebel down the hall. Although they'd never been here, his dog seemed to know right where to go. She ran up to Kensie's unit and sat on the welcome mat, then thumped her tail frantically.

Before he caught up to her, the door swung open and Kensie was standing there. She wore workout gear and carried a yoga mat under her arm, which fell to the ground as soon as she saw Rebel. Her gaze darted up, eyes comically wide as they met his.

He smiled, but it was shaky. "Hi, Kensie."

Rebel lifted her front paws off the ground, almost knocking Kensie over as she rested them on Kensie's forearms.

"Rebel," Colter admonished, but it lacked heat. He wanted to jump on Kensie himself.

Kensie laughed and dropped to her knees, wrapping her arms around Rebel's neck as his dog's tail swung back and forth. "Hi, Rebel." She looked up at Colter. "Her leg healed well."

"It's as good as it will ever be," Colter agreed. The same as his. Neither of them were quite whole, but then again, if they were good enough for a woman like Kensie, maybe they didn't need perfect.

Finally Kensie stood, wariness in her gaze. "What are you doing here, Colter? I thought—"

"You thought I'd never leave Alaska?"

She laughed, but it sounded more like nervous energy than amusement. "Sort of. I figured the next time I saw you would be when Desparre thawed out and I could get back up there."

"It's not enough," he told her. "Phone calls for six months."

She bit her lip and the hand petting Rebel sped up.

"Can I come in?" he asked, not wanting to have this conversation in the hallway.

"Sure. Of course." She snagged her yoga mat off the ground as she spun, her hand shaking as she held the door for them.

Her apartment was just like he'd expected it to be, with bright, happy colors and—if you angled your head just right—a view of the water. But he didn't give it much of a look, because he couldn't take his eyes off Kensie, staring back at him like she was afraid of what he'd come all this way to tell her.

He set his cane against the wall. He hadn't needed it for weeks. "How's your sister?"

She looked thrown by the question, probably expecting him to dive right into the question of their relationship. "It hasn't been easy. She's still adjusting. But my family feels whole again, Colter." She clutched her hands together, betraying her nerves as she added, "No matter what, I'll always be grateful to you for helping bring her home."

Not wanting to draw out why he'd come and make them both anxious, Colter started at the beginning. "Rebel and I have been traveling across the country for the past few weeks."

"What?" She sank onto the couch, shaking her head. "I don't understand. We've been talking. You were in Alaska."

"No. I just didn't want to tell you about it until I was finished." He sat on the chair next to her, taking her hands in his as Rebel scooted her way between the couch and the coffee table to lie on Kensie's feet.

"Rebel and I made a journey to see the families of each of my brothers."

"Oh, Colter," Kensie breathed, squeezing his hands tighter.

"It's something I've been meaning to do since that day. Something I haven't been able to bring myself to do. First, it was the injury and then it was guilt. Guilt over being alive when they were all gone." His voice cracked, but he forced himself to continue. "I always felt like it wasn't fair for me to move on when none of them would ever have a chance to do it. But you know what every single one of those families told me?"

"What?" she asked softly, lifting one hand to swipe away the tears he felt on his cheeks.

"I was dishonoring their memories by refusing to live my life." He took a deep breath, trying to get control of his emotions. "And my life is you, Kensie."

Her eyes widened even more, the nervousness that had filled them before replaced with hope.

"And then Rebel and I went to see my family."

Her eyes filled with tears at his words. She knew he hadn't seen them since he moved to Alaska.

"It was tough. They still don't understand me, but they love me. And they're happy about what I'm doing now."

"What's that?" Kensie whispered, her eyes still huge.

"I found a nonprofit organization that wants my experience. I'm going to be helping others like me, coming out of the military. Or families who need support after facing loss. It's downtown."

She blinked a few times, looking confused. "Desparre has a nonprofit downtown?"

He grinned. "Not in Desparre, Kensie." He squeezed her hands tighter, hoping he wasn't moving too fast, springing this on her instead of talking it over first. "Downtown Chicago."

Her mouth moved a little, like she wanted to speak, but didn't know what to say, so he rushed on.

"I'm looking at an apartment across town this afternoon." He'd wanted to be as close to her as possible, but he couldn't afford anything near the waterfront. Not yet.

"That's…" She shook her head. "You don't need to look for one. You can stay with me."

His heart picked up speed, not from nervousness now, but excitement. "Your place doesn't allow pets. I pretended Rebel was a service dog to get her up here, but I'm not sure how long that will—"

"No," Kensie interrupted. "I'll move. Wherever you want. I mean, I can't go to Alaska. I would, if things were different. But my sister—"

"I know." He cut her off, hardly able to believe she was saying *yes*. That she was going along with his crazy plan—even upping the ante—after knowing him barely more than a month.

"I'm going to keep my cabin in Alaska. I'm hoping we'll visit. And the city isn't easy for me. I didn't just pick Desparre because of the solitude, but also because it helps with my anxiety. I'll probably need some help adjusting. But I want to," he added when it looked like she was going to say something. "I want to deserve you."

She scooted closer to him and Rebel lifted her head off Kensie's feet, staring up at her as if she knew something important was happening.

"Are you kidding? How could you not deserve me? You brought me back my sister. You saw me for *me*. You're *here*."

He smiled, so much joy inside him it was hard to breathe. He couldn't remember the last time he'd felt this way, but he knew it was before that fateful day he thought he'd lost everything.

But she was wrong. He didn't deserve her. Not yet. He needed to reclaim his life to be the man she deserved in hers. And he wasn't there yet. But with her help—and her love—he knew he could do it.

Kensie shifted closer still, until she was almost hanging off the edge of the couch. In response, Rebel scooted backward, out from between the couch and table. She ran around the edge of the room, so she could force her way between Colter's chair and where Kensie sat.

Colter laughed as Rebel rested her head on his arm, her gaze going back and forth between him and Kensie, tail wagging faster and faster.

"I guess we should start apartment hunting," Kensie said. Her voice was full of wonder and surprise, but it was also filled with love.

In that moment, he knew without a doubt he'd made the right choice.

"It doesn't matter where we end up," he told her. "You're the only home I'll ever need."

At his words, she launched herself off the couch and onto his lap, throwing her arms around his neck. "I love you, Colter," she breathed.

He barely had time to respond before she was kissing him.

Beside them, Rebel barked her approval.

* * * * *

Get 4 FREE REWARDS!

We'll send you 2 FREE Books plus 2 FREE Mystery Gifts.

Harlequin® Romantic Suspense books feature heart-racing sensuality and the promise of a sweeping romance set against the backdrop of suspense.

FREE
Value Over
$20

YES! Please send me 2 FREE Harlequin® Romantic Suspense novels and my 2 FREE gifts (gifts are worth about $10 retail). After receiving them, if I don't wish to receive any more books, I can return the shipping statement marked "cancel." If I don't cancel, I will receive 4 brand-new novels every month and be billed just $4.99 per book in the U.S. or $5.74 per book in Canada. That's a savings of at least 12% off the cover price! It's quite a bargain! Shipping and handling is just 50¢ per book in the U.S. and 75¢ per book in Canada.* I understand that accepting the 2 free books and gifts places me under no obligation to buy anything. I can always return a shipment and cancel at any time. The free books and gifts are mine to keep no matter what I decide.

240/340 HDN GMYZ

Name (please print)

Address   Apt. #

City   State/Province   Zip/Postal Code

Mail to the **Reader Service:**
IN U.S.A.: P.O. Box 1341, Buffalo, NY 14240-8531
IN CANADA: P.O. Box 603, Fort Erie, Ontario L2A 5X3

Want to try 2 free books from another series! Call **1-800-873-8635** or visit www.ReaderService.com.

Get 4 FREE REWARDS!

We'll send you 2 FREE Books plus 2 FREE Mystery Gifts.

Harlequin Presents® books feature a sensational and sophisticated world of international romance where sinfully tempting heroes ignite passion.

FREE Value Over **$20**

YES! Please send me 2 FREE Harlequin Presents® novels and my 2 FREE gifts (gifts are worth about $10 retail). After receiving them, if I don't wish to receive any more books, I can return the shipping statement marked "cancel." If I don't cancel, I will receive 6 brand-new novels every month and be billed just $4.55 each for the regular-print edition or $5.55 each for the larger-print edition in the U.S., or $5.49 each for the regular-print edition or $5.99 each for the larger-print edition in Canada. That's a savings of at least 11% off the cover price! It's quite a bargain! Shipping and handling is just 50¢ per book in the U.S. and 75¢ per book in Canada.* I understand that accepting the 2 free books and gifts places me under no obligation to buy anything. I can always return a shipment and cancel at any time. The free books and gifts are mine to keep no matter what I decide.

Choose one: ☐ **Harlequin Presents®** **Regular-Print** (106/306 HDN GMYX) ☐ **Harlequin Presents®** **Larger-Print** (176/376 HDN GMYX)

Name (please print)

Address   Apt. #

City   State/Province   Zip/Postal Code

Mail to the **Reader Service:**
IN U.S.A.: P.O. Box 1341, Buffalo, NY 14240-8531
IN CANADA: P.O. Box 603, Fort Erie, Ontario L2A 5X3

Want to try 2 free books from another series? Call 1-800-873-8635 or visit www.ReaderService.com.

HP19R